LADY JUSTICE

AND THE
ABDUCTION

A WALT WILLIAMS
MYSTERY/COMEDY NOVEL

ROBERT
THORNHILL

1

Lady Justice AND THE ABDUCTION

Published in the United States of America

1. Fiction, Humorous
2. Fiction, Mystery & Detective, General

LADY JUSTICE AND THE ABDUCTION

CHAPTER 1

I had just hung up from talking to Kevin McBride, my partner in Walt Williams Investigations, verifying the fact that we currently have no clients and that the prospects of getting one in the near future were bleak.

Given the fact that we are both in our mid-seventies, this wasn't necessarily bad news. We take cases when they come along, but when there are none, it's not the end of the world.

My wife, Maggie, still an active real estate agent, was out with buyers. Having nothing better to do, I decided to take a quick snooze.

I had just stretched out when I heard someone banging on the door.

"This better be important," I muttered, somewhat miffed that my nap had been interrupted.

My heart sunk when I opened the door and saw Jerry Singer, my tenant from the first floor of our three-story building.

Jerry is a great guy and I love him dearly. He's like one of our family, but he has one very annoying trait. He fancies himself a stand-up comic and is always bending our ears with his corny jokes. He makes a weekly appearance at the Comedy Club on amateur night and it's not uncommon for him to run his material by one of us before his performance. I cringed, figuring that was the purpose of his visit.

"Jerry, what can I do for you?"

"I'd like to invite you and Maggie to the Comedy Club tonight."

Swell, I thought. A *whole evening of corny jokes*.

"Oh, are you performing tonight?"

"No, this is lady's night at the club."

"Then, why ---?"

He blushed. "There's someone I'd like you to meet. She's performing tonight."

That caught me by surprise. "Is this lady someone special?"

He blushed again. "I guess you could say that --- I think she is."

Jerry had my attention. I had known the little guy for ten years. He was approaching seventy, and to my knowledge, had never shown any interest in women --- or men. This was definitely a side of Jerry I hadn't seen before.

My curiosity overcame my reluctance. I definitely wanted to see the gal that had lit Jerry's fire.

"What's her name?"

"Dixie."

"Sure, we'd love to come. What time?"

"She comes on at seven."

"We'll be there."

Maggie got home about four-thirty. At seventy-five, she's still active, but no spring chicken. She kicked off her shoes and collapsed in the recliner.

"Eight houses! They liked them all but can't make up their minds. I'm bushed. How about ordering pizza, then you can rub my feet while we watch TV?"

"Would you settle for two out of three?" I asked, taking off her shoes.

She sighed. "Which one won't I get?"

"The TV. We've been invited out for the evening."

Maggie's mouth dropped open when I told her about my visit with Jerry.

"A woman? Jerry wants us to meet a woman?"

"Yep. Apparently he has the hots for this gal at the comedy club. I know, it took me by surprise too. Are you in?"

Maggie's curiosity overcame her fatigue. "I wouldn't miss it for the world."

CHAPTER 2

We arrived at the comedy club at six-thirty.

Jerry met us at the door and escorted us inside.

"I saved you a table right up front," he said, proudly.

When we arrived at our table, I was shocked to see Georgia Peach and Granny Smith at the next table.

I had met Georgia and her partner, Wanda Wanger, a few months ago. They are bounty hunters and fate had thrown us together on several occasions. Kevin and I had actually saved her life twice. In appreciation, Georgia's mother, Elberta, had invited Maggie and me to their house for dinner on two different occasions.

To say that their family was interesting would be an understatement. The family names, Madison, the father, Elberta, the mother, Bonita, the sister, and Melba, Bonita's daughter, like Georgia, were all named after varieties of peaches. Granny Smith, the only apple in the family, turned out to be a classmate of my tenant, Bernice Crenshaw.

"Georgia! What are you doing here?"

"Hey, Walt. We came to see my aunt. She's performing tonight. How about you?"

I leaned over and whispered, "We're here with Jerry. He's sweet on one of the women performing. He wanted us to meet her."

"Oh, really. Which one?"

"I think he said her name is Dixie."

I saw the look of astonishment on Georgia's face. "Dixie is my aunt!"

Now I was the one astonished. "You've got to be kidding me!"

"Nope!" She pointed to Granny Smith. "Dixie is Granny's older daughter."

Then I thought about our two meals at the Peach household. "I'm surprised we didn't meet her when we came to dinner at your house."

Georgia rolled her eyes. "Unfortunately, Aunt Dix isn't welcome there."

"How come?"

"Well, Aunt Dix has always been the black sheep of the family. You've met my mother, so you know she's pretty straight-laced."

That was definitely an accurate assessment of Elberta Peach. She was the embodiment of June Cleaver, the wholesome housewife.

"Anyway," Georgia continued, "Mom never wanted her around. She said it would be a bad example for Bonita and me."

"What in the world did she do?"

"For starters, she quit school. Then, in the late 60's and early 70's she was a stripper at The Folly on 12th Street."

I remembered the old Folly Theatre. During its heydays, it featured Gypsy Rose Lee, Tempest Storm, and Chesty Gabor --- or so I've been told.

"After the Folly shut down, she hooked up with a magician and toured as his girl Friday. We lost track of her for a while, then learned that she was running with Sammy 'Scarface' Spalitto, an Al Capone wannabe. After Sammy was sent to prison for armed robbery, she went to California and got bit parts in B movies. When she got too old for the Silver Screen, she started doing stand-up comedy, and here we are."

"My goodness! She does have a colorful past." I pointed to Granny Smith. "How did Granny take all that?"

Georgia smiled. "She's a mom, and moms love their kids no matter what."

And from what I had seen of Granny, she could be a bit naughty herself.

I felt Jerry tap me on the shoulder.

"Walt! She's about to come on."

I turned to Georgia. "Talk to you later."

The house lights dimmed and Phil McCrevasse, the owner of the club, took the mike.

"Ladies and gentlemen, hold onto your hats! The Comedy Club is proud to present Dixie Red, the crusty comedienne."

As the audience applauded, I leaned over to Georgia. "Dixie Red. Isn't that ---?"

She rolled her eyes. "Yes, that's the name of a peach."

I should have known. The rest of the family had peach names. Why not Dixie?

I watched Jerry as Dixie took the stage. He was grinning from ear to ear.

I was a bit surprised when I saw her. She was tall. At least six inches taller than Jerry. She reminded me of a cross between Lily Tomlin and Allison Janney. Although obviously getting up in years, I could see that in her younger days she must have been quite a looker.

"Good evening! I'm so happy I could be here with you this evening --- actually, at my age, I'm just happy to be anywhere. When I got up this morning, I looked in the paper. When I saw that my name wasn't in the obituaries, I knew it was gonna be a good day.

"I'll tell you one thing. Old age isn't for the feint of heart. Over the years, things change. One day I realized I could laugh, cough, sneeze, pee, and fart, all at the same time. Then there's the hot flashes. I thought that was all behind me. Then one day, I thought I was having another one but it was a false alarm. It was just one of my boobs in my coffee cup."

A woman a few tables over laughed so hard she snorted her drink out her nose.

"And dating at this age. Let me tell you, it's no fun. No fun at all. I'm sure you remember the seven dwarfs, Doc, Happy, Sneezy, Sleepy, Dopey, Grumpy and Bashful. Well, as they've aged, there's still Dopey, Grumpy and Sleepy, but Doc, Sneezy, Happy, and Bashful have become Wrinkly, Saggy, Leaky, and Farty.

"A friend of mine set me up on a blind date. Everything was going fine. After dinner I invited him up to my place hoping for a little hanky-panky, if you know what I mean.

Unfortunately, it was then I realized I'd spent the evening with Saggy. You'd think a guy would know that there's pills for that.

"Since that didn't work out, she set me up with another guy. As soon as I got in his car, I knew she'd set me up with Farty. In the movies, he was constantly squirming. 'Sorry,' he said. 'My butt's asleep.' 'I know,' I replied, 'I can hear it snoring!'

"Thank you, ladies and gentlemen. You've been a great audience!"

There was a thunderous round of applause.

Jerry turned and gushed, "Isn't she great!"

I nodded. "Indeed she was." And definitely crusty. She lived up to her billing.

After a quick break, she joined us at our table. We had invited Georgia and Granny Smith to sit with us.

She gave Jerry a peck on the cheek and hugged her mother and niece. "All my favorite people right here together."

Jerry pointed to us. "Dix, I'd like you to meet my best friends, Walt and Maggie."

She shook our hands. "Pleased to finally meet you. Jerry has told me so much about you."

"Likewise," I replied. "We really enjoyed your set."

"Yeah," Granny chimed in. "It was a real pip!"

For the next hour, we chatted. I was surprised to see that Dixie was quite the opposite of her on-stage persona. We found her quite engaging, polite, and funny. I could see why Jerry liked her. At the end of the evening, one thing was very clear --- my old friend Jerry was definitely smitten.

CHAPTER 3

Sammy Spalitto watched Dixie's performance from the back of the room. It had been twenty-five years since he'd seen her, but he could vividly recall that fateful day when he got busted for robbing the bank.

Dixie was driving when he told her to pull up in front of the First Bank of Kansas City at 39th and Main. She had no idea she was to be the wheel man in the robbery.

Sammy wasn't aware that a teller had activated a silent alarm. By the time he had filled his satchel with money, a lone police car was converging on the bank.

He remembered tossing the satchel in the back seat and screaming at Dixie, "DRIVE! DRIVE!"

It was soon apparent that Dixie was no match for the officer in the black and white. Sammy ordered her to pull to the curb where he bailed out and ran. The lone officer elected to pursue the fleeing Sammy. Twenty minutes later, he was in cuffs.

That was the last time he saw Dixie or the thirty thousand in the satchel.

After her performance, Sammy saw her join some people at one of the tables. He saw her give a small, geeky-looking guy a kiss on the cheek. He grinned. If that schmuck was her latest squeeze, there wouldn't be a problem.

It was an hour before the small group rose to leave the Comedy Club. Sammy didn't mind the wait. It had been twenty-five years. Another hour was no big deal.

He followed them to the parking lot. Dixie gave the geeky guy another smooch and headed to her car.

He followed her into the garage of one of the old garment buildings downtown that had been converted to lofts. As she stepped out of her car, he confronted her.

"Hey, doll. Long time, no see."

A feeling of dread spread through Dixie's body as she recognized the apparition from her past.

"Sammy?"

"Yes, it's me all right, and we need to have a conversation about my thirty grand."

Two days after our evening at the Comedy Club, I was at my desk paying bills when there was a knock on the door.

It was Jerry.

"Walt! I'm worried!" he said, barging in the door.

"Whoa! Slow down. Worried about what?"

"Dixie! I think something's happened to her."

"Why do you think that?"

"She was supposed to come to the Comedy Club last night to catch my act. We were going to grab a bite afterward, but she never showed. I tried to call but it went straight to voice mail. I tried again this morning. Same thing. Something's just not right."

"I'm sure there's a reasonable explanation," I replied, trying to reassure him. "Have you talked to her family? Maybe they know something."

"Uhhh --- no. I didn't think of that"

I pulled out my cell phone. "I'll give Georgia a call. Maybe she's heard from her."

Georgia answered on the first ring.

"Walt! I was just about to call you. Can you check with Jerry and see if he's heard from Dixie? She's not answering our calls."

Now I was starting to worry.

"Actually, that's why I was calling you. Jerry is here with me now. He hasn't been able to reach her either."

"I've got a bad feeling about this," Georgia said. "What do you think we should do?"

"Do you know where she lives?"

Jerry tugged on my sleeve. "I do"

"In a loft downtown," Georgia said.

"Okay then. Let's start there. Jerry and I will meet you."

Georgia was already there when we pulled into the parking garage.

"Look!" Jerry said, pointing. "That's her car."

"Maybe that's a good thing," I said, hopefully as Georgia joined us. "Maybe she just fell asleep in her apartment."

"Or she fell and can't get up," Jerry said. "She gets around, but she's no spring chicken."

"Only one way to find out. Let's go."

We paused outside the door to her apartment and knocked. No answer.

"Do you have your picks?" Georgia asked.

I thought I'd try a Kevin response to lighten the mood. "Is Rodney Dangerfield disrespected?"

Georgia looked at me like I was some kind of nut. "What?"

Jerry grinned. "I think that's a yes."

Georgia rolled her eyes. "Everyone's a comedian."

I pulled out my picks and went to work. The locks in this newly refurbished building were more sophisticated than any I'd tried before.

"Maybe we should call Kevin," Jerry said as I fumbled with the picks.

"Be patient!" I replied, exasperated at my ineptitude. "I'll get this."

It took fifteen minutes, but I finally heard the 'click.'

Georgia pushed the door open. "Aunt Dix! It's Georgia. Are you here?"

Silence.

Let's look around," she said.

We checked every room. No Dixie.

"Well," I said, "there was no sign of forceable entry and nothing's torn up. It doesn't even look like she's been here."

"But her car!" Jerry said. "Maybe something happened to her in the parking lot."

I was about to reply when Georgia said, "Take a look at this. It's a scrap book."

"Wow! This is so cool," she said. "These are posters from her days dancing at the Folly."

There was a photo of the old theatre during its burlesque years and a play bill featuring Lois DeFee, the 6' 4" Amazon. Dixie Red was also billed as the opening act.

On the following pages were photos of playbills featuring Mandrake the Magician.

"That's Dixie!" Georgia gushed, pointing to an attractive woman seemingly being levitated by the marvelous Mandrake.

On the next page was a newspaper article dated August 16th, 1995.

The headline read, *BANK ROBBER APPREHENDED.*

The story went on to say that Sammy Spalitto robbed the First Bank of Kansas City and was apprehended when he leaped from his car and tried to escape on foot. It said that Spalitto's accomplice escaped along with the money stolen from the bank.

The article also carried a photo of Spalitto being led away in cuffs.

I stared at the photo for a moment. "I've seen this guy somewhere. Let me think."

Then it came to me. "Now I remember! He was at the Comedy Club the other night. I noticed him because he was sitting alone at a table in the back of the room. I don't think I saw him smile even once. He was much older, of course, but I'm sure it was the same guy!"

"That explains a lot," Georgia said. "I'll bet he followed Dixie home and abducted her in the garage."

I had a thought. "This is a fairly new complex. I wonder if they have surveillance cameras in the garage?"

We headed to the building's rental office.

The receptionist looked up from her console. "How may I help you?"

"We'd like to speak to the building manager," I replied.

"Have a seat. I'll see if Mr. Simpson is available."

A moment later she returned with a middle-aged man.

"I'm Carl Simpson, building manager. What can I do for you?"

I handed him my card. "I'm Walt Williams, private investigator. I'm hoping you can help us. Do you have surveillance cameras in your garage?"

He nodded. "As a matter of fact, we do."

"I was hoping we could see your footage from two nights ago."

"What's this all about? I can't just show surveillance information to anyone off the street. We must protect our tenant's privacy."

"That's why we're here. One of your tenants has disappeared and we have reason to believe she was abducted from your parking garage. If you'd rather, we can go to the police and have them come take a look, but if word got out that your parking lot was dangerous, I imagine you'd have a difficult time renting those vacant units."

He stared at me for a moment. "Two nights ago? What time?"

"Let's say between ten and eleven."

We followed him into his office and he fiddled with the video controls.

"Okay, here's ten P.M. I'll fast forward until we see something."

At ten-thirty-five, Jerry pointed. "There! That's her car."

We watched as another car pulled up behind her. A man got out and confronted her. We could see as the look of surprise, then shock, registered on her face.

After a brief conversation, the man grabbed her by the arm and shoved her into his car. When he turned, we could see his face clearly.

Dixie had been taken by Sammy 'Scarface' Spalitto!

CHAPTER 4

"Should we call the police?" Jerry asked. "Or the FBI? Dixie's been kidnapped!"

Having been a cop for five years, I knew that the police weren't going to do much based on the video we'd just seen.

"I'll give Ox a call," I replied, trying to placate Jerry.

Ox was my partner during my five years on the force. More than once after retiring I'd called on him for help on a case.

"Hey, Walt. What's going on?"

"Hi partner. I could use a favor."

"What a surprise. What is it this time?"

"I'd like you to run a name, Sammy Spalitto, and see what you can tell me about him."

"I guess I could do that without getting into too much trouble. I'll call you back."

While we were waiting for his call, we went back to Dixie's apartment and continued to look through Dixie's scrapbook. Following the article about Sammy's arrest, were playbills of B movies in which she'd had a small part. Following those were playbills where she'd performed her comedy act.

"Your aunt has had quite a career," I said as Georgia closed the book.

Before Georgia could reply, my phone rang. It was Ox.

"Sammy Spalitto," he said. "He got twenty-five years at Leavenworth for armed robbery. He was released three days ago."

"Is there any information on his whereabouts?"

"Nope, nothing. He's not on parole. He served his twenty-five, so he's free as a bird. Why the interest?"

"We think he may have kidnapped someone we know."

"What can I do to help?"

I thought for a moment. "Nothing now, but we'll keep in touch."

After I hung up, Georgia said, "What now? Where do we start looking?"

"I might know someone who can help," I said. "Carmine Marchetti."

Georgia's eyes grew wide. "The head of the Kansas City mafia? That Carmine Marchetti? How could he help us with Spalitto?"

"Carmine knows things. He's got eyes and ears all over the city. If Sammy's back in town,

I'd bet most anything that Carmine knows about it."

I opened my phone and hit a button.

Georgia's mouth dropped open. "You've got him on speed dial?"

I shrugged.

"Carmine. Walt Williams here."

I punched the speaker button on the phone.

"Walt! How's my favorite gumshoe?"

"Still kicking. I'd like to ask you a question."

"Ask away."

"What do you know about Sammy 'Scarface' Spalitto?"

"I know he's a putz. Thought he was a tough guy and tried to take down a bank. He bungled the job and was sent to Leavenworth. Why the interest in a schmuck like him?"

"He got out three days ago and we think he kidnapped a friend of ours. Any idea where we might find him?"

"Tell you what," he replied, "I'll pass the word to my contacts on the street. Somebody's bound to have seen him. As soon as I hear anything, I'll let you know. And Walt --- if you need any help nailing this guy, you let me know. Capisce?"

"Thanks, Carmine. I appreciate it."

Georgia grinned. "That was amazing. I'm impressed. But where do we go from here?"

"I have no idea," I replied. "Let's just hope Carmine can come up with a lead."

After checking the ties that bound Dixie to a chair, Sammy bent close and looked her in the eye.

"Okay, doll. Let's talk about my thirty grand. What did you do with it?"

Dixie stared right back. "I wanted nothing to do with your stolen money. You scared me to death. I had no idea you were going to rob that bank. If you hadn't bailed out of the car and if the cops had caught us together, I would have been in prison too."

"You're not answering my question. What happened to the money? Did you spend it?"

"Like I said, I didn't want anything to do with that money. I figured if I tried to spend any of it, the cops could somehow trace it back to me. All I wanted to do was get out of town before the cops realized I was your accomplice. I stashed the money and took off for California."

That took Sammy by surprise. "You stashed it? Where?"

"In my house. I unscrewed the grate on the cold air return, put the money inside, and screwed the grate back on. As soon as it was hidden, I was on my way west."

Sammy smiled. "I'll bet it's still there."

"Get real," Dixie replied. "It's been twenty-five years. Surely someone's found it by now."

"I guess we'll never know until I look. What was the address and what room did you hide it in?"

"Someone's probably living there. You can't just barge in to their home."

"Yeah, I can. I've been thinking about this day for twenty-five years. Maybe if they're lucky they won't be home. If they are, too bad. Now give me that address before I have to hurt you."

We waited for Carmine's call in Dixie's loft just in case she miraculously returned home. Two hours later, Carmine called back.

"Walt! Carmine here. I got an address for you. One of my guys knew Sammy back in the day. He heard that when Sammy got out of the joint, he headed for his momma's house. The old gal kicked the bucket a few years ago and with Sammy in the slammer, the house has just sat vacant. It's in bad shape, but it was a place for Sammy to hang until he got on his feet."

"Thanks, Carmine. I owe you."

"Do you want some back up? I'll send Vito."

"No, the cops may get involved so you'd better stay clear of this one, but I appreciate the offer."

"I hear ya. Good luck and don't get shot. I don't want nothin' to happen to my favorite gumshoe."

After getting the address from Carmine, I called Ox.

"Are you and Amanda anywhere close to 12th and Lister? I think we know where Sammy took our friend. We could use some back up."

"We can be there in fifteen minutes."

I turned to Jerry and Georgia. "Let's go get Dixie."

We arrived at the house on Lister just as Ox and his partner, Amanda, pulled up.

Carmine was right. The house was a wreck. The front lawn was tall weeds and trash. Most of the windows had been broken and there was a hole in the roof.

Ox was surprised to see Jerry and Georgia.

"Who is this friend that's supposed to be in there?" he asked.

"Her name is Dixie. She's Georgia's aunt and Jerry's girlfriend."

"Wow!" he replied. "I'm really behind. You'll have to catch me up when this is over. How do you want to handle this?"

"If Sammy Spalitto is in there, he may be more willing to respond to a cop. How about you and Amanda take the front. Georgia and I will go around back."

"What about me?" Jerry protested.

"You wait right here!" Ox ordered. "Let's go."

Georgia and I waded through the weeds and climbed onto the back porch. A moment later, we heard Ox bellow.

"Sammy Spalitto! This is the Kansas City Police. Open the door!"

A moment later, he called out again.

Hearing nothing, Georgia said, "I'm going in!"

Before I could stop her, she crashed through the back door. I was right behind her, just hoping that Spalitto wasn't lying in wait.

Ox must have heard the crash and hit the front door just as we entered the living room. In the corner, we found Dixie, gagged and bound to a straight chair.

"Aunt Dix!" Georgia cried. A moment later, she was freed.

Jerry came running in. "Dix are you all right?"

"I'm okay," she replied, giving him a hug. "Thank you all for coming."

"Where's Sammy?" I asked, "and why in the world did he kidnap you."

Dixie sighed. "It's a long story."

In the next fifteen minutes, she told us about her role in the bungled robbery.

"I got away with the stolen money and as soon as Sammy got out, he came looking for me. He wanted to know what happened to it."

"So what did happen to it?" Georgia asked. "Did you spend it?"

"Absolutely not! I wanted nothing to do with it. I hid it away and headed for California."

"You hid it! Where?"

31

"Behind the grate in the cold air return of the house I was renting."

"Do you think it could still be there?" Georgia asked. "It's been twenty-five years."

"I have no idea," Dixie replied, "but Sammy has gone there to find out."

"Oh, crap!" Ox said. "That means whoever is living there now is in danger. Let's go! I hope we're not too late!"

When we turned onto the street where Dixie used to live, we saw two cop cars with their lights flashing.

"Oh my God!" Dixie wailed. "We're too late! Sammy's hurt someone and it's all my fault."

We pulled to the curb just as another police vehicle arrived. It was Detective Blaylock and he was amazed when he saw the three of us plus Ox and Amanda.

"What in the world are all of you doing at my crime scene?" he asked, bewildered.

"It's a long story," I replied. "What happened here?"

"Some mope tried to break into this house and the occupant shot him dead."

That caught us all by surprise. "Sammy's dead?"

"Sammy?" Blaylock asked. "Sammy who? How do you know this guy?"

"It's Sammy 'Scarface' Spalitto," I replied. "He just got out of Leavenworth three days ago." I pointed to Dixie. "He kidnapped this woman. Ox and Amanda helped us free her, and here we are."

Blaylock sighed. "Something tells me there's a lot more to this story."

"If we can go inside," I said, "we might be able to clear this up."

"Okay, let's go. This better be good."

When we went inside, we saw an elderly man sitting on the couch.

An officer standing beside the man said, "Detective Blaylock. This is Wilbur Hawkins. He shot the intruder."

"Mr. Hawkins," Blaylock said, "Can you tell us what happened?"

"Shore can," he replied. "I was just sittin' on my porch havin' a beer and this guy comes into my yard. I figured he was some kind of salesman, so I told him to skedaddle. He said was comin' in my house and I said, 'the hell you are.' I pulled my Smith & Wesson and told him to get the hell off my lawn."

As soon as he said that, I remembered Clint Eastwood saying the very same words in the movie, *Gran Torino*.

"What happened then?" Blaylock asked.

"When he saw my piece, he turned tail and ran, but he said he'd be back."

"Do you have a permit for your gun?"

"Hell yes I got a permit. This neighborhood's gone to hell. There's drive-by shootings and I hear gunfire almost every night. Those hoodlums better think twice before they mess with me." He pointed to the body on his living room floor. "Same with this guy. He shoulda listened. I came back inside and stretched out for a nap. I heard someone on my porch and a minute later, he comes bustin' in. He shouldn't have done that."

"Do you have any idea why he wanted to come into your house?"

"Don't know and don't care. All I know is that he won't be botherin' me no more."

"I think I might know." I volunteered. "Mr. Hawkins. Do you have a step ladder and a screwdriver?"

"On the back porch. I'll fetch 'em for you."

"What the hell?" Blaylock said, perplexed.

When Hawkins returned, I placed the ladder under the cold air grate, climbed up, and unscrewed the grate.

Everyone watched as I reached into cold air shaft.

"Got it!" I said, and climbed down with a canvas bag.

I opened the bag and there it was --- thirty-thousand dollars.

"Oh my God!" Dixie muttered. "It was still there after all these years."

"Okay," Blaylock said. "Now you have my attention. Someone tell me what's going on here."

Dixie told her story from the day of the bungled robbery to being abducted by Spalitto.

When she was finished, Jerry asked the obvious questions. "Is Dixie in any kind of trouble and what happens to the money?"

Blaylock thought for a moment. "The statute of limitations has long expired. Even if it hadn't, I doubt Dixie would be in trouble. She was coerced into her role as a getaway driver. As for the money, again, the statute of limitations has expired. Plus, the First Bank of Kansas City went belly up in 2009. It doesn't exist anymore. I really don't care what happens to it."

"Well, I want no part of it," Hawkins said. "I don't need it. I got everything I need right here." He turned to Dixie. "I guess it's all yours."

She looked at the money. "I don't know. It just doesn't seem right. It was stolen!"

"Look at it this way, Aunt Dix," Georgia said, "he coerced you into committing a felony, then you had to flee to California to get away from Sammy and today, he kidnapped you. Think of it as compensation for the mental anguish he's put you through."

Dixie looked around and we all nodded.

"Well," she said, "I could sure use it."

"Then it's settled," Blaylock said, handing Dixie the bag.

"Not quite," Hawkins said. He turned to Blaylock and pointed to the body. "Would you mind gettin' this garbage out of my livin' room?"

CHAPTER 5

About a week after our encounter with Sammy Spalitto, I was outside retrieving my morning paper when Jerry came busting out the door, nearly knocking me to the ground.

"Whoa! Slow down! Where are you off to in such a hurry?"

"Sorry," he said, picking up my paper. "I'm just excited."

"So I see. What's going on?"

"I'm helping Dixie move. She took the money from the robbery and bought five acres with a double wide trailer out east of Independence."

"Really? What brought that on?"

"She was just tired of city living. Plus, she was creeped out about getting abducted in her apartment. She said she was through moving around and wanted to put down some roots."

"Can't say I blame her," I replied. "Say 'hi' to her for me --- and have fun!"

He grinned. "Oh, I intend to!"

I was happy for my old friend. I sometimes wondered why he never dated, but figured it was none of my business. As it turned out, he just hadn't met the right woman yet.

A week or so later, Kevin and I were commiserating in my office when the phone rang. An obviously distraught Georgia Peach was on the line.

"Walt! We need to talk!"

"Sure, what about? Another fugitive apprehension gone bad?"

"No, nothing like that."

"Then what?"

"I --- can't --- not over the phone. Can I come to your office?"

"Of course. Kevin is here. Is that okay?"

"Absolutely! I need all the help I can get on this one. I'll be right over."

"What was that all about." Kevin asked as I hung up.

"It was Georgia. She was upset about something she didn't want to discuss on the phone. She's coming over."

"Any ideas?"

"Not a one. With Georgia, it could be anything."

Fifteen minutes later, Georgia was in my office. I could see right away that something was terribly wrong. Her eyes were red and her face as flushed.

"I --- I just don't know what to do," she stammered.

"Just take it easy," I said, patting her hand. "Just start at the beginning."

She took a deep breath and nodded. "It's Aunt Dix. She's been abducted."

"Again!" I asked. "How many ex-con boyfriends does your aunt have?"

"No, no! It's nothing like that."

"Okay, I'm listening. Who took her this time?"

Georgia bit her lip and grimaced. "Aliens."

Needless to say, I was speechless.

"Come again," Kevin said. "I must not have heard you right. Surely you didn't just say that your aunt was abducted by aliens."

Georgia bristled. "Yes! That's exactly what I said."

"Right!" Kevin scoffed. "And *Time Magazine* just named me 'Sexiest Man of the

Year.' If this is some kind of joke, I'm not amused."

"It's no joke!" Georgia replied, and I could see the fire in her eyes.

She rose from her chair. "I thought I could count on you two, but I guess I was wrong. I'm out of here."

"Just hold on," I said, easing her back into her chair. "Just give us a minute to get our heads around this thing. You have to admit, what you've just dumped in our laps is --- uhh --- quite unusual. Tell us what happened."

"Okay," she said, glaring at Kevin, "but no smart-ass wise cracks."

Kevin raised his hands in mock surrender. "Sorry, you just took me by surprise. Please go on."

"Aunt Dix called this morning. I could tell by the sound of her voice that something was wrong. She asked if I could come to her trailer and bring Granny Smith. I asked her why. She just said she needed us and would explain when we got there. I picked up Granny and we headed to Independence.

"When we got there, Dix looked like she had seen a ghost. I think she was in shock. When we went inside, she hugged us both and broke

41

down crying. It was awful. I've never heard anyone cry so hard.

"After she had settled down some, I asked what had happened. When she responded, she had a far away look in her eyes."

"They took me," she said, and started sobbing again.

"When I asked her who had taken her, she grabbed my arms. 'Aliens! Aliens took me.'

"My reaction was like yours. I just couldn't believe it. My first thought was that she'd gotten ahold of some tainted wacky weed and had a bad trip. She's been known to smoke a joint or two.

"Then I saw the frightened look in her eyes. 'You believe me, don't you? Please tell me you believe me!'

"I asked her to start from the beginning and tell me what had happened. She did, and the story she told was absolutely --- I don't know how to describe it --- unbelievable --- frightening --- surreal."

"Well, don't keep us in suspense," Kevin said, when she faltered.

"No," she replied, resolutely. "It's not my story to tell. It won't mean as much coming from me. In order for you to believe what happened, you must hear it from the one who experienced it."

"Where is Dixie now?" I asked.

"She's at her trailer. Granny Smith is with her."

"Lead the way. Kevin and I will follow."

Although skeptical, I couldn't wait to hear from the abductee herself.

On the way to East Independence, I told Kevin everything I knew about Dixie, our night at the Comedy Club, Jerry's infatuation, her abduction by Sammy Spalitto, and her checkered past as stripper, a second banana in a magic act, and an actress in B movies.

"Wow!" Kevin said. "That's quite a resumé. Do you think there's any chance that she's made this whole thing up to enhance her stand-up comedy routine?"

"I can picture her being introduced as the Abducted Comic. It would lead to a whole new repertoire of jokes. 'A guy had his first UFO experience. He walked into the kitchen and said, 'Good morning fat-ass.' The next thing he knew, there were flying saucers coming from everywhere.'

"Then there's, 'What's the difference between a UFO and an honest politician? It's possible that UFO's actually exist!'"

I rolled my eyes. "Are you through?"

"Yeah, I guess. But you didn't answer my question."

"Do I think she's making it up? No, I don't. I can't fathom what actually happened, but from what I know of Dixie, this isn't some kind of gag. You heard how Georgia described what happened when they went into her trailer. You just don't do that to your family for shits and grins."

We had taken 24 Highway east through Independence, then turned north on Blue Mills Road.

"Hey," Kevin said. "Isn't this the road we were on when we were searching for that parcel of land from the Civil War?"

"One and the same," I replied.

After we passed the Little Blue Trace Trail, the land was sparsely populated. I knew from Jerry that Dixie had purchased a trailer on five acres in the country, but I didn't realize it was so remote.

Eventually, Georgia turned off the paved road onto a gravel driveway that led to Dixie's double wide.

We parked and followed Georgia onto the front patio. She knocked gently, then opened the door and peered inside. Seemingly satisfied, she pushed the door open and motioned for us to follow.

We found Dixie on the couch holding a steaming cup in her hands. Granny Smith was snuggled beside her.

"How's she doing?" Georgia asked.

Before Granny could answer, Dixie said, "I'm okay --- now. I was just so rattled --- being here by myself after what I went through."

She smiled when she saw Kevin and me. "When you woke up this morning, I'll bet you never saw this coming."

That was the Dixie I knew.

"That's an understatement. Do you feel like telling us what happened?"

"Actually, I want to. I want to tell the whole thing while it's fresh in my mind. Promise me you'll keep an open mind."

I raised three fingers. "Scout's Honor. We promise."

I saw the wistful look in her eyes as she began to recall her frightening experience.

"I had just finished supper and the sun was starting to set. I went out to the back patio to watch. The sunsets are so beautiful out here. It had just sunk below the horizon when I noticed a bright light shining through the trees. At first, I thought it was just some kind of reflection of the sun on the clouds, but it kept getting brighter.

"Eventually, the light was above the tree line and seemed to be coming closer. When it reached my back pasture, I could see that it was some kind of disk with flashing lights. When it started to land, I figured it was time to get the hell out of Dodge, but for some reason, I couldn't move.

"The thing landed, a door slid open, and a figure emerged. It was shaped like a man, but it wasn't a man. It was maybe five feet tall, very slim, but with an oversized head. Its eyes were large and slanted. Very black.

"As it approached, it didn't speak, but somehow I understood that it meant me no harm."

"Some kind of mental telepathy?" I asked.

"Yes, I think that would describe it. Even though I was led to believe it didn't want to harm me, I was scared to death when I was slowly lifted off my feet and swept into the disk.

"Once inside, I was placed on some kind of exam table. My arms and my feet were bound to the table. At that point, I was scared out of my wits. I had seen enough science fiction movies to know that this was the point where they would begin poking me with sharp instruments and drilling holes in my head.

"The thing must have sensed my fear. It again reassured me that they meant no harm. I was given to know that they were interested in me because of my age. They had taken and studied other younger specimens and had made note of their physical characteristics. Their interest in me was to determine how those characteristics had changed over time.

"They had strange instruments that they ran over my body. I felt no sensation until the creature placed his hands on my head. That's when everything changed. Suddenly, it was if I knew and could see everything that the creature knew and had seen. It was amazing. It was just fleeting while his hands were on my head, but I wished it had been longer. The things I saw were so --- amazing! I keep saying that, but they were!"

"Collective consciousness," I said. "Just like the Borg."

"The what?" Kevin asked.

"The Borg. In Star Trek. They were an alien race in which every member was linked to every other member by a collective consciousness. Everyone knew what everyone else knew. Captain Picard was part of the collective for a few episodes."

"Really, Walt?" Kevin said. "A TV show?"

"No," Dixie said. "He's right. That's exactly what it felt like. I seemed to know what it knew for that short time."

I stuck my tongue out at Kevin.

"Very mature," he muttered.

I turned my attention back to Dixie. "What happened then?"

"After it touched my head, everything went black. I must have passed out. The next thing I knew, I was back on my patio. Then I saw the disk. There was a flash and it was gone. It was like it had never happened. I actually wondered if I had fallen asleep and dreamed the whole thing. I still might have doubted except for what they left behind."

"They left something behind? What?"

"Come with me and I'll show you."

We walked out the back door and she led us to the grassy field behind the trailer.

"There!" she said, pointing.

In the grass was the indention of a perfect circle.

"That's where it landed," she said. "Right there!"

We all just stood there with our mouths hanging open. Finally, I had the presence of mind to grab my camera and take a photo. I wanted to preserve the evidence before a heavy thunderstorm washed it away.

"Now do you believe me?" Dixie asked, "or do you think I came out here and stomped the grass as some kind of gag?"

"No --- no," I stammered. "I don't think you did this. It's just so --- bizarre!"

"No kidding," she replied, sarcastically. "If you really want to see bizarre, try being levitated into some kind of flying saucer and probed by strange creatures."

"Let's go back inside," I said. "I'd like to know more about what you saw when the creature touched your head."

Once we were seated inside, Dixie closed her eyes and tried to recall what she had seen through the eyes of her captor.

"I saw a desert," she said, "out in the middle of nowhere. It was some kind of air base. There were planes and runways."

"Area 51," Kevin said. "I'd bet my Social Security Check."

Dixie continued. "The next thing I knew, we were inside and I could tell we were somewhere underground. There were people working everywhere. What was so strange, they were working with creatures just like the ones that had taken me. There was a saucer-like thing down there. It was similar to one that landed out back. I saw it all just for an instant and when he removed his hands, it all went away."

"Do you remember anything else?"

She thought for a moment. "No, it was shortly after that when I was taken back to my patio. What do you think it all means?"

"I have no idea," I replied, but I have some friends who might. Do you have any problem with me sharing your experience with them?"

"No, of course not. Anything to help make sense of what just happened to me."

"Great! I'll contact them and get back to you as soon as I know something."

As Kevin and I rose to leave, Georgia stood up. "I hate to go, but my partner, Wanda, and I have a couple of fugitives to apprehend. I'll find somebody else if you need me here."

"Heaven's no," Dixie replied. "I'm fine now. Go do your bounty hunter thing."

"I'm staying," Granny said. "I want to be here if those things come back. Maybe they'd like to get a look at me. That would be a real pip."

As we headed to our car, it occurred to me that the morning had been a real pip for all of us.

CHAPTER 6

On our way back to town, I thought about Kevin's response to what Dixie had seen.

"You jumped right on that Area 51 thing. Do you know a lot about it?"

He nodded. "Remember, I spent thirty years in Phoenix. Area 51 is in Nevada. Anyone who has lived in the desert for any amount of time has heard the stories about Area 51."

"Isn't that the place where the military was supposed to have taken the remains of an alien craft that had crashed?"

"That's the place. July, 1947. The crash was reported on a ranch near Roswell. Immediately, the military swooped in, scooped up the remains, and transported it to Area 51. The interesting thing is that the government's first response was to verify that it was actually the remains of an extraterrestrial craft. Here, let me show you."

He punched some buttons on his phone.

"Here's the story in the local paper."

"What happened next is really bizarre. Shortly after the story was published, the military retracted it and said that the crash was nothing more than a weather balloon."

He punched more buttons on his phone.

"This is the government's official photo of what they wanted the public to see."

"Not a spaceship, just a weather balloon."

"What about her seeing aliens working underground at Area 51? That seems a bit far-fetched."

"Yes and no," he replied.

He punched more buttons on his phone.

"This is an ariel photo of Area 51."

"The base itself, about 83 miles from Las Vegas, is six miles long and ten miles wide and sits under 575 square miles of restricted air space. It is one of the most highly classified and restricted places in the country.

"Anyone trespassing risks being shot on sight. One of the stories about the place is that there is actually more underground than what you can see from the air.

"In 1989, a fellow by the name of Bob Lazar claimed to have worked in Sector 4 which was underground and connected to a vast underground rail system that connected to other clandestine government sites. He said they were working to reverse engineer an alien spacecraft. The government, of course, denied everything and claimed they had never heard of Bob Lazar."

"Typical government," I replied. "Deny, deny, deny."

"Not just deny," Kevin said. "After they retracted their story, they contacted not only the rancher who found the wreckage, but also everyone in Roswell that had heard the story. They were told in no uncertain terms that if they ever spoke about a saucer crash, they would be arrested for treason.

"And get this!" Kevin added. "The government didn't even acknowledge until 2003 that Area 51 even existed."

I thought for a moment. "So, are you saying there could be some truth to what Dixie saw?"

He shrugged. "All I know is there are a lot of things going on that the government doesn't want us to know about. By the way, who are these friends you're going to tell about Dixie's experience?"

"Nicholas Thatcher and Arnie Goldblume."

"Ahhh, of course," Kevin said. "The Watchers."

"If anyone knows about secret government programs, it's them."

As we pulled up in front of my building, Jerry was just coming out onto the front step.

"Oh, crap!" I muttered. "Jerry doesn't know! Should we tell him?"

"Come on, Walt. If Maggie had been abducted by strange creatures, wouldn't you want to know?"

I sighed. "You're right, of course. How do you think he'll take it?"

"Only one way to find out," he said, opening his door.

"Hey, guys," Jerry greeted as we approached the front stoop. "Anything exciting going on? Are you working on any big cases?"

"Actually," I said, hesitating, "we are, and it concerns someone you know."

"Oh really? Who?"

"Dixie."

I saw the look of concern on his face. "Please don't tell me some other creep from her past has shown up."

"No, nothing like that."

"Well, what then?"

"Georgia came by this morning with some disturbing news. Dixie apparently had a --- uhh --- close encounter of the third kind."

He thought for a moment. "Close encounter of the third kind. Surely you're not saying that she's been hanging out with space guys."

I nodded. "That's exactly what I'm saying."

He burst out laughing. "Good one! You had me there for a minute. Really, what have you two been doing?"

"It's not a joke, Jerry. We've just come back from Dixie's trailer. Evidently she was abducted last night."

"Okay, you've had your fun, but enough is enough."

"Jerry! I'm serious. Something landed behind her trailer last night and took her aboard. It's quite a story. I'm sure she'll tell you everything."

He grabbed my arm. "Walt! You're my friend, but this has gone too far."

When I didn't respond, he looked into my eyes. "You aren't kidding, are you?"

I shook my head.

"My God! Is she all right?"

"She's fine," I replied, trying to reassure him. "It was a frightening ordeal, but she wasn't hurt. Granny Smith is with her."

He let go of my arm. "I gotta go!"

"Well, that could have gone better," Kevin said as we watched Jerry jump into his car and speed away.

I thought about my reaction when Georgia told me about Dixie's encounter. We've all seen movies and TV shows about alien abductions, but that doesn't happen in real life, or does it?

CHAPTER 7

I first encountered the Watchers several years ago when I was approached by Homeland Security to participate in an undercover operation to expose what they feared was a cell of U.S. based terrorists.

Homeland Security had intercepted a series of emails containing the words 'bomb' and 'dirty.' Naturally, they feared they had uncovered a plot to deploy a 'dirty bomb' on American soil.

Much to Maggie's chagrin, I infiltrated the group and met its leaders, Arnie Goldblume and Nicholas Thatcher.

As it turned out, the Watchers were the farthest thing from a terrorist organization. Arnie and Nick met when they both participated in a lawsuit against Merck Pharmaceuticals. Both of their fathers had perished taking the drug, Vioxx, which was subsequently pulled from the market.

Since both had lost their fathers due to a product that had been approved by the FDA, they became suspicious of pretty much everything government related.

Using the money they were awarded in their lawsuit, they organized the Watchers whose purpose was to keep tabs on the government.

Much to the embarrassment of Homeland Security, Arnie and Nick had set up the suspect emails using the sentence, "I dropped my bomb pop on the ground getting it all dirty." Their objective was to expose a secret government program called Echelon whose purpose was to spy on the communications of American citizens.

As a result of the investigation, Nick and Arnie became my good friends and have been very helpful in several of my investigations.

Anytime I have questions about some kind of government cover-up, it's a good bet the Watchers will have the inside scoop.

I dialed their office on Rockhill Road, just a stone's throw from the UMKC campus and the Nelson Art Gallery.

"Watchers. Arnold Goldblume speaking."

"Arnie, Walt Williams here."

"Walt! Good to hear from you. Is this a social call or have you encountered some new life-threatening issue?"

"The latter, I'm afraid. Do you guys know anything about extraterrestrials?"

He laughed. "We might know a thing or two."

"Do you have time to see me?"

"For you, Walt, always."

"I'll be right there."

"Have a seat, Walt," Nick said. "Arnie said you were interested in extraterrestrials. What's that all about?"

"I'll get around to that, but first, I'd like to know what you know --- from the government perspective. Is there really evidence that we've had visitors from outer space?"

Arnie thought for a moment. "From the government's point of view, everything probably started with the event in Roswell, New Mexico."

"I don't mean to interrupt you," I said, "but Kevin filled me in on the Roswell thing. He used to live out west, so I know about the military saying they found debris from a saucer, then reneged a few days later saying it was just the remains of a weather balloon. What happened after that?"

Arnie continued. "Then you also probably know that the military has never changed its story. According to them, no flying saucer crashed in the desert.

"Nevertheless, from that point on, the public had been awakened to the possibility that there actually was a crash and the government had covered it up. Strange sightings that had previously gone unreported were now coming in at an alarming rate. So many that the government couldn't just ignore them. Have you ever heard about Project Blue Book?"

I shook my head. "I can't say that I have."

Arnie opened a file cabinet and pulled out a manila folder. "Project Blue Book was initiated in 1952. Its stated purpose was twofold: To determine if UFO's were a threat to national security and to scientifically analyze UFO-related data.

"Over the next 17 years, they investigated 12,618 UFO reports. When the project was disbanded in 1969, they issued the following statement:

No UFO reported, investigated, and evaluated by the Air Force was ever an indication of threat to our national security.

There was no evidence submitted to or discovered by the Air Force that sightings categorized as 'unidentified' represented technological developments or principles beyond the range of modern scientific knowledge.

There was no evidence indicating that sightings categorized as 'unidentified' were extraterrestrial vehicles.

"They even went so far as to say that UFO sightings were generated as a result of:

A mild form of mass hysteria.
Individuals who fabricate such reports to perpetuate a hoax or seek publicity.
Psychopathological persons
Misidentification of various conventional objects.

I couldn't believe what I was hearing. "Not one! Not even one out of twelve thousand? Sounds like another government cover-up to me."

"Of course it was," Arnie replied. "Nick and I have read some of the eye witness accounts of UFO sightings. We're not talking about weird guys wearing tin foil hats. We're talking

Air Force pilots, law enforcement officers, and upstanding citizens."

"But why?" I asked. "Why did they feel they had to hide the truth?"

He shrugged. "Several reasons. First, remember this was the 1950's. We were in a cold war with Russia. Everyone was afraid of the bomb. Little kids were taught to hide under their school desks during drills. At first, military leaders weren't convinced that what was being seen wasn't superior Russian technology. Thankfully, President Truman put that fear to rest.

"Besides that, government officials just didn't think the public was ready to accept the idea that we weren't alone in the universe. To accept that fact would change so many things, history books, not to mention religion."

"So, was that the end of it?" I asked. "No more investigation by the government?"

"No," Arnie replied. "Quite the contrary. There were so many additional sightings, not just in the U.S., but all over the world, that in 2007, the government launched the Advanced Aerospace Threat Identification program. This was an unclassified and unpublicized investigatory effort funded to the tune of $22 million dollars. It lasted five years and was terminated in 2012."

"So, what were their findings?"

"Damned if I know," Arnie replied. "Nothing was ever released, but they must have found something. In 2013, a new program titled, the Unidentified Arial Phenomena Task Force was launched and exists still today."

"And I suppose they haven't come to any conclusions either."

He smiled. "You got that right. The government has never admitted that there are extraterrestrials visiting the earth and they probably never will."

"What about you?" I asked. "Do you believe?"

"I do. The evidence is overwhelming. There isn't a doubt in my mind that we've had alien visitors for thousands of years."

That took me by surprise. "Thousands of years! I thought you said it all started with Roswell."

"What I said was that government involvement in UFO sightings began with Roswell. Actually, there is a huge volume of evidence that aliens have been interacting with human beings for thousands of years."

Arnie pulled another file from the drawer.

"I'm going to show you photos of places you are no doubt familiar with."

The first photo was of the pyramids in Egypt.

"Just one of these pyramids, The Great Pyramid of Giza, stands 481 feet tall. It is comprised of 2.3 million stone blocks, some weighing as much as 80 tons. They are red granite which was mined 600 miles away. No mortar was used in its construction, yet the cuts on the stones are so precise it is impossible to slip a piece of paper between them. The pyramid is aligned perfectly with the North, South, East and West axis."

"The next photo," he said, "is the Pyramid of the Sun in Mexico."

"It stands 216 feet high and measures 720' by 760' at its base.

"The next one is the Stonehenge in England."

"Most of these stones weigh in excess of 25 tons and were mined in Wales, 150 miles away.

"The next one shows the monoliths on Easter Island.

"There are over 1,000 of these amazing relics, some weighing up to 86 tons.

"And finally, one of the most amazing of all, the Kalisa Temple in India."

"This amazing structure is the oldest and largest monolith in the world. A monolith is something carved out of a single piece of stone rather than stones being brought and placed together. Believe it or not, that magnificent structure was carved from the side of a mountain, starting at the top and working down. It is estimated that over 400,000 tons of rock had to be carved away to complete the temple.

"Now, what do you suppose all of these wonders of the ancient world have in common?"

I shrugged. "I have no idea, but I'm hoping you're about to tell me."

"All of them were constructed thousands of years ago, supposedly with primitive stone tools. Huge blocks of stone weighing 80 tons were supposedly transported hundreds of miles before the invention of the wheel.

"Historians would have us believe that these primitive cultures were capable of these amazing feats, but if you study ancient texts and murals, it is much more likely that these people were aided by technology from extraterrestrial visitors. I could show you dozens of pictographs describing extraterrestrial contact with early cultures. Here are just a couple."

I just sat there, trying to let everything he had said sink in.

"I just don't get it. If all that proof is out there, how can people deny the fact that we're not alone in the universe? How can people deny that we're being visited by extraterrestrials, and why hasn't someone written a book compiling all of this evidence?"

Arnie grinned. "If I remember correctly, someone did write a book about the government's clandestine chemtrail program. How has that worked out?"

"It was like preaching to the choir. It was readily accepted by those who already believed in the chemtrail conspiracy, but pretty much ignored by everyone else."

"Precisely!" Arnie said. "If the government says they're not spraying us with chemicals, then it must be true. If the government says there's no such thing as visitors from outer space, it must be true.

"Actually, there was a book written about all this. Have you ever heard of *Chariots of the Gods* by Erich von Däniken?"

"It rings a bell, but I've never read it."

"It was written in 1968. *Chariots of the Gods* posits a variety of hypotheses dealing with the possibility of extraterrestrial beings influencing ancient technology. Von Däniken suggests that some ancient structures and artifacts appear to represent higher technological knowledge than is presumed to have existed at the times they were manufactured. Von Däniken maintains that these artifacts were produced either by extraterrestrial visitors or by humans who learned the necessary knowledge from them."

"Well, there you go!" I said. "How was it received?"

"Even though it achieved best seller status, many scientists and historians rejected his ideas claiming they were based on faulty evidence. Nevertheless, his work spawned other endeavors. The documentary series, *Ancient Aliens*, on the *History Channel*, is based on his work. You should look it up. It's quite convincing."

"Okay," Nick said. "Your turn. Something must have spawned your interest in extraterrestrial visits. What have you gotten yourself involved in this time?"

I took a deep breath and told them everything I knew about Dixie and her abduction. Arnie and Nick listened intently.

"Wow!" Nick said when I had finished. "That's just too cool. So what now?"

"That's the reason I came to see you two. If we assume this actually happened, what should be our next step? Should we report it to this Unidentified Arial Phenomena Task Force or to Homeland Security?"

Arnie and Nick exchanged a worried look.

"Neither!" Arnie said, emphatically. "The best thing to do is just keep this whole incident under wraps. The fewer people who know about it, the better."

"But why?" I asked, perplexed. "I don't understand."

"Remember what I told you about the findings of Project Blue Book?" Arnie asked.

"The government says there's no such things as extraterrestrial visitors. They'll do anything to make sure nothing changes that. Also, remember we said that we had read the transcripts of interviews with Air Force pilots and other who had reported sightings?"

I nodded.

"Well, guess what? After those interviews were classified and marked 'top secret,' an alarming number of people who had been interviewed mysteriously disappeared or were killed in some tragic accident."

Arnie's words sent chills up my spine. I remembered how Jack Carson and a handful of others who were about to publish information about the chemtrail conspiracy mysteriously disappeared.

"Thanks," I said, getting to my feet. "That's exactly what I needed to know. I need to get back to Dixie and make sure she keeps her mouth shut."

Poor Dixie had endured enough problems in her life. The last thing she needed was to be stalked by government assassins!

CHAPTER 8

I didn't have Dixie's phone number but I knew Jerry was heading that way. I dialed his number but it rang and rang, eventually going into voice mail.

I stepped on the gas and hoped I would get back to Independence before someone spilled the beans.

As I turned into Dixie's driveway, I realized I was too late.

Vans from the three local TV stations and one from the *Kansas City Star* filled the front yard.

Dixie was on her front step holding court with a half-dozen microphones pointed in her direction.

I spotted Jerry standing behind the row of reporters and pulled him aside.

"Jerry! What in the world is going on here?"

He smiled. "Publicity, of course. Dixie's finally getting the exposure she's always wanted."

"Why in heaven's name would she do that?"

He looked at me like I was some kind of moron. "You're kidding, right? Think about it. Dixie's always been on stage, but always a second banana. Second billing as a stripper, girl Friday to a half-assed magician, an extra in B movies, and now amateur night at the Comedy Club. This is her big break. A chance to finally be in the spotlight."

A spotlight that might get her killed, I thought.

I pushed through the line of reporters.

"That's all folks. This interview's over. Please leave and give Dixie some privacy."

Dixie looked at me like I'd just drowned her kitten.

"Walt! What are you doing? I wasn't finished yet."

"Yes, you are!" I whispered emphatically. "I'll explain later."

"Who the hell are you?" one of the reporters bellowed.

I cringed as Jerry spoke up. "That's Walt Williams. He's a private investigator."

Suddenly, all of the microphones were pointed at me.

"Mr. Williams! What's your interest here? Why are you cutting off our interview? What is it that you don't want us to know?"

"No comment!" I said, urging Dixie back inside the trailer.

She reluctantly complied and moments later the three of us were safely inside.

Jerry, along with Granny Smith, peeked out the window. "Wow! Those reporters are really pissed."

"Not half as pissed as I am!" Dixie hissed. "This was my big moment. You had no right to come barging in like you did. What gives?"

"Let's all calm down and take a breath," I said. "I had a very good reason for what I did. Just give me a chance to explain."

After everyone was seated, I shared my conversation with Nick and Arnie.

When I finished, I saw the look of concern on Dixie's face.

"Are you telling me that my life might be in danger? That the government, the United States government, might send an assassin to keep me from telling my story?"

"All I'm saying is that for the last seventy years, the government has proclaimed that there's no such thing as extraterrestrial visitors. If they thought for a minute that an old gal like you could prove them wrong --- no, even worse --- prove that they had been lying, what do you suppose they would do?"

She thought for a moment. "Oops! I see your point. What should I do now?"

I looked out the back window and saw the reporters taking photos of the circle where the craft supposedly landed.

"I have no idea. One thing's for sure. The cat's out of the bag."

"What if I went out and told the reporters that I made it all up?" Dixie asked, wringing her hands.

"I doubt they'd believe it," Jerry replied. "You were pretty convincing. That would be like trying to put the toothpaste back in the tube."

Granny Smith had been listening intently. "I know what I'm gonna do!" she said resolutely. "I'm gonna get me a gun. One just like Bernice wears on her ankle. Ain't nobody gonna hurt my little girl!"

Great! I thought. *Another armed granny with cataracts.*

The next morning, I opened the *Kansas City Star* and there it was.

The headline read: *Independence Woman Claims To Have Been Abducted By Aliens!*

The accompanying article gave a graphic description of Dixie's ordeal complete with photos of her and the crop circle.

I had just finished reading the article when the phone rang. It was Arnie Goldblume.

"Hey Walt. Arnie here. I see you didn't get back to your friend in time."

"No, I was too late. Any suggestions?"

"I just wanted you to know that her story has caused quite a stir among UFO enthusiasts. There's been a lot of chatter online."

"What does that mean?"

"It means that if the UFO people are chatting about her abduction, then Washington knows about it too. They regularly monitor these groups looking for stories just like this one."

"What can we do?"

"Not much you can do. Just tell your friend to watch her back."

Just moments after I hung up with Arnie, the phone rang again.

It was my half-brother, Mark Davenport.

My father was as over-the-road trucker in his youth. He had a wandering eye, and like the proverbial sailor, he had a girl in every port.

Mark Davenport was the result of a dalliance he had with a truck stop waitress in western Kansas. She never told my dad about his offspring and I might never have known I had a sibling had he not shown up unexpectantly at my door. At that time, he was with the FBI and was interested in a case I had been working on.

Since that chance meeting, we have grown reasonably close. He has since transferred to the office of Homeland Security and we have actually worked together on several cases.

"Mark, good to hear from you. I hope this is a social call. I'm getting too old to wrangle with terrorists."

"I wish it was, Walt, but I'm afraid this is official business. It's regarding Dixie Smith. I saw the footage of you at her trailer."

That took me by surprise. "How is that possible? I was never on any of the TV news reports."

"I saw you on the raw footage before it was edited for TV."

"How could you possibly ---?"

"Let's just say we have our ways and that I've seen it. How do you happen to be mixed up in this thing?"

"Do you remember Jerry?"

"Of course. The funny little guy who tells jokes."

"Well, Jerry met Dixie at the Comedy Club and was smitten. He invited Maggie and me to the club to see her act. It turned out that she was the aunt of another acquaintance, Georgia Peach."

"The bounty hunter?"

"One and the same. Anyway, after Dixie's encounter, Jerry dragged me out there. That's how I got involved."

"Unbelievable! So what's your take on this whole thing?"

"Before I answer your question, answer one for me. Why is Homeland Security interested in an old woman in Independence, Missouri?"

"I think that would be obvious. If one of our citizens is abducted, it could be a potential threat to national security."

"Oh really? I thought the government's official position is that there is no such thing as extraterrestrials?"

A long pause.

"Come on, Walt. Are you going to bust my chops on this? A little cooperation would be appreciated."

"Let me remind you that you guys don't have the best track record around here. Jack Carson and five others mysteriously disappeared when they were about to expose the government's chemtrail conspiracy. And how about Dr. Skinner's mysterious box? As soon as you guys knew he was working on the Neuron Encoding Synapse Disruptor, a team was sent to confiscate it."

"You know that was a rogue agent."

"Yes, but an agent none the less. By the way, I know about Project Blue Book too, and I know that many of the people who reported sightings to the government also disappeared. Is that what you folks have in mind for Dixie? Make her disappear so the world won't find out that the government has been lying to us all these years about extraterrestrial visitors?"

"Wow!" Mark said, "you've really got your panties in a twist over this one. I'm guessing by your reaction that you must give some credence to her story. Look, all I want to do is talk to her. You can be with me when I do. My job is to assess any possible threats to our country. One hour and I'll be on my way. I promise."

"It's not you I'm worried about, Mark. If you talk to her and find her story credible, it's who is coming after you that concerns me."

"All I can do is give you my word. Will you help me?"

I sighed. "I'll talk to Dixie and see if she's willing to meet you. I'll let you know either way."

"Thanks, Bro. I appreciate it."

After hanging up from Mark, I gave Dixie a call. I had gotten her number on my last visit.

"Hi Dixie. Walt here. I'd like to stop by for a chat if you're up to it."

"Sure, come on over."

Forty-five minutes later, I was in her living room.

"Okay," she said, "what's so important to bring you all the way out here?"

I told her about my conversation with Mark.

She looked at me in disbelief. "Are you serious? Homeland Security wants to talk to me?"

I nodded. "They do. UFO groups have picked up your story. Homeland Security monitors those groups. That's how they found out about you. They just want to be sure that what happened to you isn't a threat to our country."

"What do you think? Should I talk to him?"

"I do trust Mark, and frankly, I don't think they're going to just let this slide. I'm thinking you might as well get it over with. I'll be right here with you during the interview."

She sighed. "I really opened a can of worms calling the press, didn't I?"

I nodded. "Yeah, you kinda did."

"Then I guess I'll do it. Let me know when and where."

I gave Mark a call. He said he'd be in Kansas City in two days. We'd meet at Dixie's trailer. He wanted to see the crop circle for himself.

As I drove home, I had a bad feeling. I trusted Mark, but he was just one guy in the huge government bureaucracy, and I doubted he would have the last word in this investigation.

CHAPTER 9

One thing that kept bothering me was something Arnie said. He said that acknowledging the existence of extraterrestrial visitors would change everything, and he mentioned history and religion specifically.

I understood the history part. During the twelve years I was in school, plus six years in college, not once were alien visitors mentioned. Even in my astronomy class in college, there was not a word about life forms coming to visit us from out in the cosmos.

Religion was something else altogether.

I know that pretty much every religion worships a deity of some kind. Surely Arnie wasn't suggesting that the deities that are worshipped by millions around the globe are actually beings of extraordinary intellect with technology far above anything we have here on earth.

I knew just the person who could give me insight into this puzzling dilemma, Pastor Bob.

I've known Bob over ten years, since the day he came into our real estate office looking for a church building. He had been the pastor of a large Protestant denomination, but had rebelled when his superiors forced him to espouse their political agenda from the pulpit.

Rather than accede to their demands, he left and over half of the congregation followed him. I found him a building on Linwood Boulevard where he established his Community Christian Church.

Pastor Bob isn't like other clerics I've known. He's sincere, but not pious, and he has a great sense of humor. He calls the church's bowling team The Holy Rollers. The sign on the outside of the church bears the quote by Martin Luther, "Sour godliness is the devil's religion."

Even though I like and respect Pastor Bob, the trappings of organized religion have never appealed to me. That's not to say that I don't believe in a higher power. I do. Even though I don't attend his services, in the past ten years there have been many times that I have needed spiritual counsel. Bob has always been there for me.

I called his number.

"Heavenly Hotline. Press 1 for English, press 2 for Latin, press 3 for Ancient Sumerian."

"Good one, Bob! I'm glad you've changed your banter. The thirty pieces of silver thing was getting old."

"Walt! I haven't heard from you in a while. Should I assume you're seeking guidance through some spiritual conundrum?"

"Something like that. Do you have some free time?"

"For you, always. I can't wait to hear what can of worms you've opened this time."

As always, the church doors were unlocked and Pastor Bob was in his office.

"Welcome, pilgrim," he said, rising and taking my hand. "How's Maggie and the rest of your crew?"

"Everyone's fine," I replied. "Thanks for asking."

"Great!" he said. "Now that the pleasantries are out of the way, what brings you to my office today?"

I took a deep breath. "Extraterrestrials. Do you believe they exist?"

His face broke out in a big grin. "Creatures from outer space. Walt, you never disappoint.

That's quite a broad subject. Could you be a bit more specific?"

"Do you remember Arnie Goldblume and Nicholas Thatcher?"

"The Watchers. Sure."

"The other day, I was discussing this topic with Arnie and he said that if and when the existence of extraterrestrial visitors was proven, it would change history and religion. What do you think he meant by that?"

"Before I answer, let me ask you the same question. Do you believe the earth has been visited by beings from outer space?"

"Considering the thousands of sightings worldwide, I'd have to say yes."

"And how long do you think these beings have been visiting our planet?"

"Well, the other day, Arnie showed me photos of the pyramids, Easter Island, and other relics that would suggest that the primitive cultures back then could not have constructed these ancient wonders. He said archeological records give credence to the idea that these wonders were either constructed by aliens or by the indigenous population using alien technology."

Bob clapped his hands. "Very good, Walt! I think you're on the right track."

"Glad to hear it. Now comes the question I've been pondering. Every major religion worships some kind of deity. Is there any chance ---?"

"That the gods we humans worship were actually ancient aliens?" he said, finishing my sentence.

"Yes, that's it exactly. How ---?"

"Walt, surely you don't think you're the first person to ever ask that question."

"Actually, I hadn't given it much consideration."

"Well, the answer is --- you're not. You said Arnie showed you some photos. I have a few myself."

He opened a file cabinet and pulled out a manila folder.

"Let's go way back in history to the ancient Greeks. This is a photo of the ruins at Delphi just north of Athens."

"It was built for Apollo, the god of music, harmony and light. Apollo was the son of Zeus, the god of the sun. The ancient Greeks worshipped many such gods. They called them 'sky gods' that came from the heavens in fiery chariots.

"To humans living 400 years before Christ, is it difficult to imagine that to them, space craft were fiery chariots?"

"That does make sense."

"Did Arnie show you the pyramids in Central America built by the Aztecs and Mayans?"

"Yes, he did. More structures that couldn't have been built by the native population."

"Exactly. These magnificent alters were to honor their deity, The Feathered Serpent. Here, I'll show you a picture."

"The Aztecs called the Feathered Serpent Quetzalcoatl. The Mayans called him Kukulkan. The feathers represented his ability to fly into the skies, and the serpent represented his ability to walk among the humans on the earth. What earthly creature fourteen hundred years before Christ could fly into the heavens?

"There are an estimated 535 million people that practice Buddhism. The Buddhist scripture states, 'In the sensuous world, there are destinations that include our own human realm as well as realms occupied by other beings.

Sermons may be given from one world to another with a flash of light.'

"Here is a photo of the largest Buddhist temple in the world located in Bangkok, Thailand."

"Tell me, Walt. What does that look like to you?"

"I think it's pretty obvious. A flying saucer."

"There are over 1.8 billion Muslims in the world, roughly 24% of the world's population. One of Islam's most holy places is the Dome of the Rock in Jerusalem. It was the original site of Solomon's temple and was built to house the Ark of the Covenant.

"The original temple was destroyed and the current one was built by the Persians. It is built over a sacred stone that was believed to be the place where Abraham attempted to sacrifice his son. Even more important, it is the place from which Mohammed left this earth and ascended into heaven. Ascended into heaven. What do you suppose that means? Here's a photo of the Dome of the Rock."

"In addition, the Bible is full of passages of beings coming to earth from the heavens riding in fiery chariots.

"I could go on, but I think you get the picture."

"So you **ARE** suggesting that many, if not most, of the beings that primitive cultures believed were gods were actually alien visitors!"

"All I'm saying is that if you look at the ancient texts of virtually every religion, their art, their statuary, their temples, it is not out of the question to suppose that beings entering their world in interplanetary vessels with advanced technology could easily be interpreted as gods descending in fiery chariots."

Needless to say, I was surprised to hear a Christian pastor even consider such a possibility.

"But --- how can you stand at the pulpit every Sunday and preach to your congregation, knowing, or at least considering the possibility, that everything that they'd been taught was wrong?"

"The answer to that is simple. Religion is not about the messenger. It is about the message, and the message I preach is to love one another, be kind to one another, and take care of one another. I really don't care where the message came from. All I know is that it's a universal truth.

"Think about this. If I stood at the pulpit and proclaimed that the deity we worship is actually an alien from a distant planet, how do you think that would go over?"

"Probably not very well."

"Exactly! Look, Walt, I'm just a guy like you. I have no idea whether any of this is true.

Maybe someday there will be convincing evidence one way or the other. In the meantime, I have a congregation of souls who look to me for spiritual guidance. I will continue to preach the message and not worry about the messenger who brought it."

I thought for a moment. "That makes sense, but let me ask you one last question. As a Christian, you believe in one all-knowing, all-seeing God. If the beings we have come to believe are gods are simply aliens from an advanced civilization, doesn't that shake your faith just a bit?"

Bob smiled. "Not at all. Who do you think created the aliens?"

He had me there.

"Okay," Bob said, "now I have a question for you. Why the sudden interest in visitors from beyond?"

"Did you see the article in the paper about the woman who claimed to be abducted by aliens?"

"I did. Quite a story."

"Well, she's a friend of mine. No, actually, she's a friend of a friend. Jerry met her at the Comedy Club, was smitten, and now they're dating."

Bob shook his head. "Unbelievable. I feel for the poor woman. I don't know which is more frightening, being abducted by aliens or being romanced by Jerry the Joker."

I had to agree. It was a toss-up!

CHAPTER 10

The next day, Mark Davenport showed up at my door a few minutes before ten.

"Hey, Walt," he said. "Are you ready to do this?"

"I am," I replied, "but I want your word that you'll go easy on Dixie. No government strong-arming. I heard about how the military threatened the people in Roswell after they covered up the truth about the crash in the desert."

"Sounds like you've been talking to some of those crazy conspiracy theorists," he said, trying to evade the issue.

I looked him in the eye. "Are you saying that's not true?"

He held up his hands. "Look, it's like I told you the other day. All I want to do is talk to her, hear her story, and if I believe what she says is not a threat to national security, I'll be on my way."

"Okay. You're my brother, so I'm going to take you at your word. Let's go."

When we arrived at the trailer, I was surprised to see several cars parked in the driveway. We knocked on the door, and when Dixie let us in, there was Jerry, Georgia, and Granny Smith.

"What's going on?" I asked. "Did I miss something?"

It was Granny Smith that spoke up. "We're here for Dixie. All of us. The minute we heard that some tight-ass from Washington was gonna grill her, we figured we'd better be here --- you know --- as witnesses."

Mark whispered. "Who's that?"

"Let me make some introductions," I said. "This is Dixie. You've already heard from her grandmother. We call her Granny Smith. This is her niece, Georgia, and you know Jerry.

I pointed to Mark. "This is my tight-ass brother from Washington. His name is Mark Davenport."

"Pleased to meet you all," he said. "If we can find some place private to talk, I'll do what I have to do and get out of your hair."

"We'll talk right here!" Granny said. "Ain't gonna be no secrets today."

Mark looked to me for help.

I shrugged. "Looks like it's all or nothing."

He sighed. "Very well." Then he looked directly at Granny Smith. "Is it okay with you if I record our conversation?"

She pulled a miniature tape recorder out of her purse. "I reckon not, since we're going to be recording it too."

Mark rolled his eyes and took a seat across from Dixie.

He clicked on the recorder, entered the date and everyone present at the interview. "Okay, Dixie. Do you mind me calling you Dixie?"

"Why would I mind?" she replied. "it's my name."

Granny giggled.

"Very well, Dixie. What I'd like you to do is just start at the beginning and tell me everything, exactly as it happened."

For the next twenty minutes, Dixie told her story just as she'd told it to me several days ago. When she got to the part where the creature put his hands on her head, Mark interrupted.

"So you're saying you think you saw things that the creature knew or had seen?"

"I'm sure of it. There were things --- beautiful and wonderful things --- that I could never have imagined even if I wanted to."

Mark continued. "You say you saw something in the desert?"

"Yes, it must have been some kind of airport. There were planes on a runway. What I saw next was underground. Creatures just like him were working on some kind of craft with men in military uniforms. It was just there for a moment, and then it was gone."

"What happened next?"

"Dixie concluded her story about passing out, then finding herself back on her porch watching the craft speed away."

"Walt said there was some kind of impression out back."

"Yes," Dixie replied. "It was where the saucer was sitting."

"I'd like to look at it."

We all followed Dixie through the trailer, out the back door, and across the lawn to the circular imprint.

"There it is!" she said, pointing.

"Interesting!" Mark said, snapping several pictures of the impressions.

Then he pulled out another device.

"What's that?" I asked.

"It measures radiation," Mark replied.

He started his examination maybe twenty feet from the impression and worked his way to the circle, making notes as he moved along.

"Well?" I asked when he'd finished.

"I'll tell you in the car," he whispered.

Then he turned to Dixie. "I think that about wraps it up. I have everything I need. Thank you for your cooperation."

"That's it?" Granny asked, suspiciously. "No lie detector test? Nothing like that?"

Mark grinned. "Granny, I think you've been watching too many sci-fi movies. Just the interview. That's all I needed, and like I promised, I'll get out of your hair now. Let's go, Walt, so these folks can get on with their lives."

I said my good-byes and we headed back to Kansas City.

"So," I said, "what do you think?"

"She certainly sounded sincere."

"That's all you have to say? What about the radiation? You said you'd tell me in the car."

"Based on the readings I took, it does appear that whatever made that impression left a radioactive footprint."

"So what now? What happens next?"

"I'll go back to Washington and file my report."

"And that will be the end of it?"

"Honestly, Walt, I don't know. It's not my call."

"That's what I was afraid of."

I had a bad feeling that there was more to come.

Three days later, a man approached Dixie's trailer and knocked.

"Dixie Smith," the man asked, handing her a card.

She nodded.

"My name is Michael Sullivan. I'd like to speak with you for a moment."

"I don't mean to be rude, but whatever you're selling, I'm not interested."

"Oh, no, Ms. Smith. Nothing like that. I'm from Washington. I just have a few follow up questions from your interview with Mark Davenport."

She looked at his card. "No one told me someone else would be coming."

The man smiled. "I apologize. It was kind of last minute. This won't take long. I promise."

She hesitated.

"Look," he said, "I understand your skepticism. Let's give Mark a call in Washington if that would make you more comfortable visiting with me."

She sighed. "No, that won't be necessary. Come on in."

"You said this was about my interview," she said after they were seated.

"Yes," he replied. "That was quite an experience. It must have been quite unsettling."

"When it happened, yes, but afterward not quite as much."

"You're a brave woman indeed! Unfortunately, not everyone is as unflappable as you."

"No, I suppose not."

"Good! I'm glad you understand."

"Understand what?"

"That what you went through could prove to be frightening to many others. I'm sure you wouldn't want innocent people to be upset by your ordeal."

Dixie gave him a puzzled look. "Why would what happened to me be of any concern to anyone else? And for that matter, why is it any of your business?"

"As I said earlier, I work for the government, and it's the government's job to protect it's citizens. There are those in Washington who believe a tale of an alien abduction could cause undue panic in many of our less secure citizens."

"So, what are you saying?"

"I'm saying that it would be better for everyone concerned if you would retract your story. We would be willing to make it worth your while."

Dixie couldn't believe what she was hearing.

"Retract my story! I can't do that! It happened! It's all true!"

"Please don't misunderstand. I'm not saying it didn't happen. What I'm saying is that it's not the best thing for the people of our country to believe that at any time they might suffer the same thing that happened to you."

"But if I take it back, it makes me look like a liar --- no, even worse, it makes me look like some kind of nut case."

"We've thought of that," Sullivan said. "You're in show business. You have a comedy act. People in show business do crazy things all the time to get noticed. I'm sure you've heard the old saying, 'There's no such thing as bad publicity.' We could say that you were just drumming up interest for your comedy routine."

She shook her head. "But that's a lie. I just can't lie."

"Like I said," he interrupted, "we can make it worth your while."

"I don't understand."

"We'll give you ten thousand dollars to retract your story and say it was a hoax."

107

Dixie was stunned. "Ten thousand!" Then she thought for a moment. "No, my good name is worth more than ten thousand dollars."

He sighed. "All right. I figured you'd be a hard sell. Let's make it twenty-five thousand. Do we have a deal?"

"Twenty-five --- I don't know. I'll have to think about it."

"Don't think too long, Ms. Smith. You have twenty-four hours. You have my card. Give me a call and I'll have the cash in your hand within an hour.

"Oh, one more thing. It's not just the money. Believe me, it would be in your best interest to accept our offer.

"Good day, Ms. Smith. I'll be waiting for your call."

The moment Sullivan was out the door, Dixie called Walt Williams.

I was taking a snooze in my recliner when the phone rang. It was Dixie.

"Walt! A man from Washington just left my trailer."

"Oh really! What did he want?"

"He offered me twenty-five thousand dollars to retract my story and say that it was a hoax."

I couldn't believe what I was hearing. "Whoa, slow down. Start at the beginning and tell me everything."

For the next fifteen minutes, Dixie told me everything she could remember about her conversation with the mysterious Michael Sullivan.

"Okay," I said when she was finished, "just sit tight and let me make some phone calls. Don't do anything until I get back to you."

As soon as she hung up, I dialed Mark.

"Mark! I trusted you!"

"Walt, I figured I'd be hearing from you."

"Damned right you're hearing from me. Who's this Michael Sullivan character. Is he one of yours?"

"No, he's not. I filed my report and hoped that would be the end of it, but evidently it got someone's attention up the ladder. Sullivan is with the CIA. What did he want?"

"He offered Dixie twenty-five grand to retract her story, and that's not all. He left a not-so-veiled threat that it would be in her best interest to accept his offer. Is that really what it's come to? The U.S. government bribing and threatening its citizens!"

"I'm so sorry, Walt. Evidently someone up the chain felt that her story was a national security risk. I hope for her sake you can convince her to accept their offer and move on."

I didn't bother to respond. After I hung up, I was so mad, I threw my phone across the room.

CHAPTER 11

The next morning, I was eating my bowl of Wheaties, the breakfast of champions, and reading the *Kansas City Star* when the phone rang.

It was Kevin.

"Walt, are you watching the news?"

"No, I'm eating my breakfast and reading my paper."

"Then turn on the TV. Channel 8 --- and hurry!"

I grabbed the remote and turned on the TV to Channel 8.

The photo of an elaborate crop circle filled the screen.

I just caught the reporter saying that the circle had been spotted in a field just east of Independence by the field's owner.

"Holy crap!" I muttered.

Then I heard Kevin on the phone which was still in my other hand.

"Walt! Did you see it?"

"I did! Amazing!"

"You know what's even more amazing?"

"No, but I'm sure you're going to tell me."

"That field adjoins Dixie's property on the east side. I saw her trailer when the traffic copter flew over it to get to the field."

"Oh brother! We need to get out there."

"My thoughts exactly. Put your pants on. I'll be there in ten minutes."

"What do you know about these things?" I asked as we headed to Independence.

"Just what I've seen on the *History Channel*," Kevin replied. "Apparently, they've shown up all over the world. There seems to be a lot of them in England, close to that Stonehenge thing."

"Makes sense. Arnie and Nick told me about the Stonehenge. Some of those rocks weigh 25 tons and were mined in Wales 150 miles away. Ancient alien theorists say there is no way the indigenous people could have built it --- at least not alone."

"I've also heard," Kevin continued, "that there are over 2,000 different patterns, many of them very complex. No doubt some have been created as a hoax, but certainly not all of them. Especially when you consider that they appear overnight."

"Why do you think this one appeared in the field next to Dixie just a few nights after she was supposedly abducted?"

"No idea."

"Well crap!" I muttered as we approached Dixie's driveway. "I was afraid of this."

The road was lined with news vans from every TV station and newspaper.

"No doubt those reporters have been trying to get to Dixie for a comment. You'd better give her a call and let her know we're coming to the door."

I called her number and it rang eight times before she picked up.

"Walt, I almost didn't answer. Then I saw your name on the caller ID. I've been getting calls all morning. I just quit answering the phone. Where are you?"

"Kevin and I are in your driveway. May we come in?"

"Of course."

Minutes later, we were inside.

"Quite a circus out there," I said, stating the obvious.

"You have no idea," she replied.

"That's quite a design in your neighbor's field," Kevin said. "Did you hear or see anything at all last night?"

She shook her head. "No, nothing. I didn't even know it had happened until a reporter came banging on my door."

Then I saw the concerned look on her face. "It has to be the aliens, doesn't it?"

I wasn't sure what to say. "It seems pretty unlikely that humans could have made an intricate pattern that large overnight without you hearing something."

She nodded. "That's what I thought. Now I have a real problem. Based on what you told me yesterday, I had decided to accept Sullivan's offer, take the money, say it was a

114

hoax, and just get this thing behind me. I can't do that now. With that thing in the field next door, everyone would know that my retraction was a lie. I would then be a liar as well as a laughing stock. I can't do that. My career would be over."

"So what are you going to do?"

"I'm going to call Sullivan and tell him, 'no deal.'"

"Would you like me to call him for you?" I asked.

"No, I'm a big girl, but I would like you to listen to the conversation."

"Of course."

Dixie picked up the phone and dialed the number on the card.

"Mr. Sullivan, this is Dixie Smith."

"Ms. Smith, thanking you for calling. I hope you have good news for me."

"I don't. Have you seen the morning news?"

"Yes."

"Then you know about the crop circle in the field next to my trailer. I was going to accept your offer, but now I can't. I'm sure you can see why."

Silence.

"I understand how the appearance of that circle might make your decision more difficult, but let me remind you that there are some very powerful people who believe your retraction is a matter of national security. Please don't worry about that circle. We have people on the way who will come up with a logical explanation for it that doesn't include alien visitors."

"So, what you're saying is that the government is going to orchestrate another cover-up."

"My goodness no. Not a cover-up, just an alternate explanation."

"Sounds like a cover-up to me. Anyway, regardless of what your people come up with, I'm not taking your offer."

"But Ms. Smith ---."

"Good day, Mr. Sullivan," she said, hanging up.

Dixie looked at me and bit her lip. "Did I do the right thing?"

In my heart I knew there was no right thing. Only time would tell if she made the right choice.

CHAPTER 12

Sullivan was true to his word.

The next day, a team arrived saying they had been dispatched by the government to investigate the crop circle.

After a cursory examination, they proclaimed that it was a hoax perpetrated by individuals looking to sensationalize the absurd claim of an alien abduction next door.

Their conclusion came as no surprise to any of us that had heard the conversation with Michael Sullivan.

After I returned home from Dixie's trailer, I called Mark Davenport, told him about the appearance of the crop circle, and Dixie's conversation with Sullivan, turning down his offer.

"Mark, his very words were, 'There are some very powerful people who believe your retraction is a matter of national security.' Do you think Dixie is in danger? I want your honest opinion."

A long silence. "Walt, it isn't just the story of being abducted that has officials concerned. People are saying that all the time. Just look at the *National Inquirer* at the grocery store check stand. It's what she reported seeing in the desert. Specifically, seeing aliens working along side the military on a strange air craft."

That took me by surprise. "Mark! Are you saying that's true?"

"No, no! Not at all! What I'm saying is that the military doesn't want the public to even think such a thing could possibly be true. Remember, about a year ago, some nut on Facebook started a page that advocated storming Area 51. The message was that they can't stop all of us. Over two million people responded that they would show up. Thankfully, on the day of the event, only about a hundred and fifty people showed up and none got into the base, but you can see the potential problem if it becomes widely publicized that we are secretly working with aliens at Area 51."

"I understand, but Dixie has promised that she won't publicize any of the details of her experience. I would hope that would satisfy those that are concerned."

Mark's reply sent chills up my spine.

"I wouldn't count on it."

I had just returned home from having lunch at Mel's Diner when I met Jerry coming out the door.

"Where are you headed?" I asked, not really caring, but wanting to be civil.

"Dixie's," he replied. "I don't like to leave her alone with all she's been through. Plus, those reporters are like rabid dogs. They just won't leave her alone."

"Is she feeling all right otherwise?"

"I guess so --- except for her foot."

That got my attention. "What's wrong with her foot?"

"Well, we don't know. Nothing that we can see. She just says that sometimes it tingles like something's inside. Kind of a weird, itchy feeling."

"When did this start?"

He thought for a moment. "Right after her abduction, I think."

Now I was really interested. "Do you mind if I tag along?"

"Of course not. The more, the merrier."

119

Dixie was surprised to see me standing beside Jerry on her doorstep.

"Walt! What are you doing here? Have you heard something from your brother in Washington?"

"Unfortunately, no. That's not why I'm here. Jerry mentioned something about strange sensations in your foot."

She scoffed. "I'm sure it's nothing. Probably just my imagination."

"Do you mind if I take a look?"

"Hey, if you get off looking at an old woman's foot, more power to you."

"Okay, but promise me you won't use this in one of your comedy routines."

She grinned. "You know I can't make a promise like that."

After we were seated, she slipped off her right shoe.

"Like I told Jerry, it doesn't hurt. It just kind of --- uhhh --- tingles sometimes."

"Not all the time?"

"No, maybe once or twice a day. It usually lasts about five minutes and then it's gone."

"And you never experienced this before your abduction?"

I saw the concerned look on her face. "No, I guess not. What are you thinking?"

"Just a shot in the dark," I replied. "Didn't you say that after you experienced the mind meld with the alien, that you blacked out?"

She thought for a moment. "That's right. The next thing I knew, I was on my back porch watching the saucer thing disappear into the air."

"So, you have no idea what might have been done to you after you passed out?"

"Not a clue. Do you think they might have done something to me?"

"It's a possibility. I've been doing a lot of reading about alien abductions since your experience. Some people who claimed to have been abducted, but not all, have reported finding implants in their bodies."

She looked at her foot. "Surely you don't ---. Well I'll be damned! That would certainly explain what I've been feeling. What else do you know about these --- implants?"

"Not much, but I know someone who will. Do you mind if I make a call?"

"Help yourself."

I dialed the Watcher's number.

"You've reached the Watchers. Arnold Goldblume speaking."

"Arnie, Walt Williams here. What do you know about alien implants in abductees?"

"Is this about the friend you were telling us about a week or so ago?"

"It is. She's been experiencing some tingly sensations in her foot since her abduction, and I thought ---."

"That she had received an implant," he said, finishing my sentence.

"Exactly! What do you know about these implants?"

He thought for a moment. "There was a Dr. Leir who claimed to have removed implanted objects from several patients. Some of the implants had strange magnetic properties, some contained odd crystalline structures, and others emitted deep space frequency radio waves.

"He sent one implant, from a patient he called Number 17, to a lab in New Hampshire for testing. The report said that it contained rare earth elements and seemed to emit electromagnetic frequencies, indicating that the object could be some kind of a communication or tracking device.

"That's about all I know."

"That's a big help, Arnie. I figured I could count on you."

"Anytime. Hey, keep us in the loop. We'd love to hear more about your friend."

"I will. I promise."

"Well," I said, hanging up. "What do you think about that?" I had turned on the speakerphone during our conversation.

"Well, it's comforting to know that others have had similar experiences and lived to tell about it. What do you think we should do?"

"There's only one way to know for sure," I replied. "Have it x-rayed."

She laughed. "Right! I'm just supposed to waltz into the emergency room and tell them I need an x-ray because I think little green men have implanted something in my body? Instead of sending me to x-ray, they'd probably escort me to a padded cell."

"Not what I had in mind," I replied. "I know a doctor. Doc Johnson. He's been treating Maggie and me for years. He has an x-ray machine in his office, he's discreet, and he's heard some pretty wild tales from yours truly. He'll do it for us."

"Hey, if he's willing, I'm willing."

I dialed Doc Johnson's office.

"I'd like to speak with Doc Johnson. I know he's probably busy, but tell him it's Walt Williams calling and I have a doozy for him."

A few minutes later, Doc Johnson came on the line.

"A doozy, huh. Is that what you told my nurse?"

"That's exactly what I told her, and I'm willing to bet a steak dinner at the restaurant of your choice that you've never had a patient like this."

"I'll take that bet. I've been doing this for forty years. I think I've seen about everything. What've you got?"

"Well, damn!" he muttered after my explanation. "There goes my steak dinner. Bring her in. I can't wait to see this."

"You heard?" I said turning to Dixie.

She nodded.

"Put your shoe on and let's go."

"Remarkable story," Doc Johnson said, examining Dixie's foot, "but I don't really see anything on the surface of your skin. Let's take a picture just to be sure."

After the x-ray, Doc punched some keys on his computer and the x-ray of Dixie's foot popped onto a viewing screen.

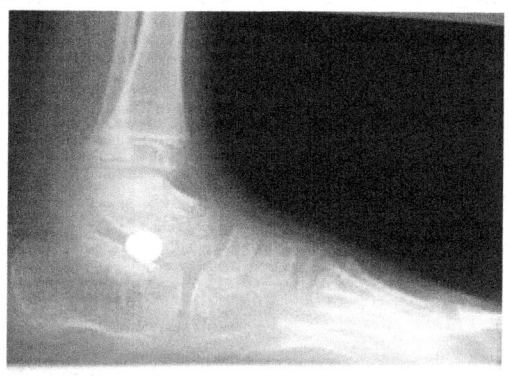

He squinted at the screen, wiped the lenses of his glasses and looked again.

"Well I'll be damned," he muttered. "There is something in there, but I don't have a clue as to how it got there."

"Any idea what it might be?" I asked, already knowing the answer.

"Nope. Not a one." Then he turned to Dixie. "Now the question is, what do you want to do?

I can remove it if you want. It would be a simple surgical procedure."

Dixie thought for a moment. "No, leave it there. It doesn't hurt and hopefully it won't kill me. Those creatures put it there for a reason and I'd like to find out why."

Doc Johnson shrugged. "Your call."

I shook his hand. "Thanks Doc. I still owe you a steak dinner for doing this for us."

"Nonsense!" he replied. "This will be another chapter in the book I'm planning to write when I retire. Maybe this will make it a best seller!"

"All right," I said as we dropped Dixie off at her trailer. "You be sure and let us know if anything changes, or if you need anything at all."

"I will," she promised.

As we drove home, I had the unsettling feeling that Dixie's unusual encounter was far from over.

CHAPTER 13

I had just finished my lunch when there was a knock on my door.

I opened the door and found myself staring at two men in black suits with narrow black ties, wearing black fedoras.

This couldn't be good.

"Look," I said, "if you guys are passing out religious pamphlets, I'm not interested."

I started to close the door, but the closest man stopped it with his foot.

"Mr. Williams, I assure you we're not passing out pamphlets."

"Well, if you're collecting for the Red Cross, I'd be happy to make a donation."

When I saw the steely look in his eyes and his jaw clench, I was reminded of a quote by Dirty Harry. "When a naked man is chasing a woman through an alley with a butcher knife and a hard-on, I figure he isn't out collecting for the Red Cross."

These guys were definitely not soliciting donations.

"Okay, then, how may I help you?"

"You're a friend of Dixie Smith."

"Yeah, so what?"

"We know you have been working with her on her alleged encounter with alien intelligence. We just wanted to ask you to cease your collaboration with her and not pursue this incident in the future."

I was beginning to get irritated. "Why would I do that?"

"Because it's a matter of national security. Surely you understand."

I nodded. "Ahh, now I get it. You're the *Men in Black*. Which one of you is Tommy Lee Jones and which one is Will Smith?"

He bristled. "If you think this is some kind of joke, I assure you that it is not. We take the security of our country very seriously. Please pass this message along to your partner, Kevin McBride and your friend, Jerry Singer. If you don't, you'll leave us no choice but to visit them ourselves. Trust me, you don't want that."

"And if I don't?" I replied, belligerently.

He pulled out his cell phone and showed me a photo of Maggie getting out of her car in front of the real estate office.

"I think it would be in your best interest to comply."

I couldn't believe what he was saying. "You're threatening my family if I don't go along with your silly game?"

"Again, I assure you, this is no game. When it comes to the security of our country, we do what we have to do. Do I make myself clear?"

"Yes, crystal clear," I said, gritting my teeth.

"Good day then, Mr. Williams. I trust it won't be necessary for us to cross paths again."

They turned and climbed down the stairs.

I just stood there, stunned. It took me a few minutes to catch my breath.

I knew to what lengths the government would go to protect its dirty little secrets. Five people who were about to blow the whistle on the chemtrail conspiracy mysteriously disappeared. There wasn't a doubt in my mind that these people would make good on their threats if we didn't comply.

I was trying to decide what to do when my phone rang. It was Georgia Peach.

"Walt! Some spooky guys just showed up at my door saying that Granny and I should just forget everything we know about Aunt Dix's abduction. What's that all about? Are they serious?"

"Yes, Georgia," I replied, "they're deadly serious. Get Granny and come to my apartment. Can you do that?"

"We'll be there in twenty minutes."

I called Kevin and Jerry and made the same request.

Thirty minutes later, everyone was gathered in my living room.

"What the heck's going on?" Kevin asked. "Why all the secrecy?"

I told him about my visit by the Men in Black. Georgia confirmed that her visit was much the same.

"Can they really do that?" Georgia asked, "just bust into our lives and tell us what we can and can't do?"

I told everyone what I knew about the deaths surrounding the chemtrail conspiracy.

"Based on what I've seen in the past, I think we have to take their advice seriously."

"How about giving your buddies at the Watchers a call?" Kevin suggested. "I'd be interested to hear what they have to say about these creeps."

"Good idea," I said, dialing their number.

"You've reached the Watchers. Arnold Goldblume speaking."

"Arnie, Walt Williams. You said to keep you informed about Dixie's abduction. Well, here's the next chapter. What do you know about the Men in Black?"

"Great movie!" he replied. "Tommy Lee Jones and Will Smith. 1997, as I recall."

"Arnie! I'm serious. Both Georgia Peach and I were visited by these guys. What do you know about them?"

"Geez! You are serious. To tell you the truth, not much. Remember, the government has never acknowledged that extraterrestrials even exist. Roswell never happened. It was a weather balloon that crashed, and so forth.

"In spite of what they say to the general public, it's pretty difficult to ignore the fact that thousands of people have reported sightings and encounters like Dixie had.

"It is rumored that the government established a secret agency to investigate everything alien related. It had to be secret, because to acknowledge its existence would be the same as acknowledging alien contact.

"The government denies such an agency exits, but enough people have been contacted by these men over the years to at least spread rumors of their existence. Hence, movies like

Men in Black. There were actually three of them, I think."

"Arnie, they threatened me. Not a veiled threat, but a direct one. I'm convinced that they're serious. Would you agree?"

"I would, Walt. Be careful. All of you."

"We will. Thanks, Arnie."

After I hung up, I turned to my friends. "Well, there you go. Any questions or comments?"

"Just one," Kevin replied. "It looks like we're out of the alien business."

Everyone nodded.

"I have one more call to make," I said, dialing.

"Mark, this is your brother, Walt."

"Hey, Walt. What can I do for you?"

"You can call off your dogs! That's what! I had a visit today from two goons from some secret government agency telling me to back off and forget about Dixie's alien encounter. They even threatened to hurt Maggie if I didn't play ball. You know who these guys are, don't you?"

Silence.

"That's what I thought," I said, hanging up.

I looked ay my circle of friends. I could tell they were as frightened as I was.

CHAPTER 14

After our encounter with the Men in Black, I had a conversation with Dixie telling her what had transpired. I told her that to insure our safety, all of us, including her family, would have to stay as far away from the alien thing as possible. She said that she understood and readily agreed not to involve any of us further.

In spite of the threats posed to her by Michael Sullivan and the threats posed to the rest of us by the Men in Black, she steadfastly refused to retract her story. She said that it happened and nothing could change that.

Jerry, being smitten, wasn't about to walk away from his new-found sweetie, but he promised not to become involved with anything abduction related.

One afternoon, about a week after my conversation with Dixie, I heard a frantic pounding on my door.

It was Jerry.

He burst into my apartment ashen-faced and out of breath.

"Walt! You'll never guess what just happened?"

"Probably not, but I'll bet you're going to tell me."

"I went out to Dixie's place. We were going to drive to the Independence Center Mall, do some shopping, then go somewhere for supper."

"Sounds like a nice afternoon."

"It would have been, but we never even made it to the highway."

"Why not? What happened?"

"The strangest thing. We took Dixie's car. She was driving. About a mile from her place, there's a big curve in the road. She stepped on the brakes to slow down, but there weren't any brakes. Her foot went straight to the floorboard.

"We were going about forty-five miles an hour and the car wouldn't stop."

"Good lord! Is Dixie okay?"

"She is. Thankfully, there was a gravel access road that led into a farmer's cornfield. Dixie swung off the road and through a barbed-wire fence. The corn was thick enough that it stopped the car about a hundred feet into the field."

The minute Jerry said, "no brakes," something clicked in my mind.

"Her car's not that old, is it?"

"Two years, I think."

I remembered several cases when I was on the force. I learned that a skillful saboteur could make a partial cut in a brake line --- not enough to go all the way through --- but enough to make the line rupture when pressure was applied. In the cases I was familiar with, the unfortunate drivers didn't survive.

"Where's the car now?"

"We had it towed to Smitty's Garage in Independence."

"Take me there," I said, grabbing my coat.

When we arrived at Smitty's, I spotted Dixie's car up on one of the racks. It didn't look too bad. The front grill was scraped where it made contact with the barbed wire fence, and a few cornstalks clung to the chassis.

A guy in overalls was fiddling with a computer.

"Excuse me," I said, "are you working on Dixie Smith's car?"

He looked up. "Shore am. What can I do for ya?"

"Uhhh, we're friends of Dixie. Have you figured out the problem?"

"Heck yes. That was easy. Brake line busted. I was just lookin' up the part number when you came in."

"Any idea what might have happened?"

He looked at me like I was an idiot. "Like I said, it was busted."

"Right, but do you have any idea WHY it busted?"

"Coulda been anything. She might have run over somethin'. Might have been a defective part."

"Is there any chance the line was cut?"

"I guess you didn't hear me. I didn't say it was CUT! I said it was BUSTED!"

I could see that I wasn't going to get any more out of the hillbilly mechanic.

"Thanks, I appreciate your time."

As we headed back to my car, I asked, "Is Dixie home?"

"Yeah, I took her back there after we dropped off her car."

"Then that's where we're going. We need to talk."

After we were seated in Dixie's living room, I took a deep breath.

"I don't want to alarm you, but I think there's something we need to consider. Your accident today might not have been an accident."

I saw the look of concern on Dixie's face.

"I don't understand."

I told them both about the cases I'd seen where the brake lines had been partially cut.

Her eyes grew wide. "You think someone deliberately cut my brake line? But why?"

"Do I really have to spell it out?" I replied. "Michael Sullivan came right out and told you that very powerful people considered you to be a risk to national security, and that it would be in your best interest to retract your story. You haven't done that.

"You have to understand that these people will do whatever they think is necessary to quell anything they perceive as a threat. They have many ways of making a death look like an accident. Cutting a brake line is just one."

"So, what are you saying? Do you think I should retract my story and claim that it was just a hoax?"

"No, I'm not saying that. That's a decision you have to make for yourself. All I'm saying is to watch your back. If this was an attempt on your life, it failed, and most likely, they'll try again."

CHAPTER 15

With the possible attempt on Dixie's life, I wasn't surprised when Jerry showed up at my door a few days later.

"Walt," he said sheepishly, "I need a favor."

"And what would that be?"

"Dixie was pretty rattled after her abduction and the thing with the brakes. She was so upset she hasn't performed at the Comedy Club since. She's doing better now. In fact, she wants to go on stage tonight."

"Sounds like the right thing to do," I replied.

"I agree, but I'm also afraid --- you know --- for her. You said it's possible that one of those government creeps might come after her again."

"It's definitely a possibility."

"Exactly! That's why I'd like you to come with us --- just in case."

I grinned. "I'm flattered that you'd think I could intimidate a government assassin, but I doubt that would be the case. I'm grey-haired, seventy-seven years old, and weigh less than a buck fifty. I'm not exactly an imposing figure."

Just the same, I'd feel a lot better if you were there."

I sighed. "Okay, but just this once."

He threw his arms around me and gave me a big hug. "Thanks, Walt. I knew I could count on you. I'll pick you up at six-thirty!"

After he left, I called Kevin. I figured if there was a possibility we could encounter an assassin or two, it might be a good idea to have back up.

The club was packed, but with Jerry's connections, he got us a seat at a front row table.

The first two comics were just okay. Nothing to write home about. The third one was Fred Firestone, one of my favorites. With his bug eyes and gravely voice, he did a great impression of Rodney Dangerfield. He had the tug at the collar down perfectly.

"I tell ya," he said, pulling at his tie. "Getting a date at my age is no picnic. I see in the audience, a lot of guys with cute chicks. Me, I get no respect.

"I tell ya, if it wasn't for pick-pockets, I'd have no sex life at all.

"The other day, I thought I had a date. She called and said, 'There's nobody home. Come on over.' So I went over and sure enough, nobody was home.

"It got so bad, I went to a psychiatrist. I told him that everybody hates me. He said I was being ridiculous. Everyone hadn't met me yet.

"I went to another psychiatrist. After hearing my story, he said I was crazy. I told him I wanted a second opinion. He said, 'Okay, you're ugly, too.'

"See, no respect at all. I went to my doctor. I said, 'Doc, every morning when I get up and look in the mirror, I feel like throwing up. What's wrong with me?' He said, 'I don't know, but your eyesight is perfect!'

He waved his hand. "Thanks, you guys are a great audience."

Dixie was scheduled to go on next. I had been watching the crowd for suspicious characters, but everyone seemed okay.

The announcer took the mike. "Ladies and gentlemen, one of your favorites is back! Please give a warm welcome to Dixie Red!"

Dixie took the mike.

"I understand exactly what Fred was talking about. Finding romance at our age is almost impossible. It's pretty sad when you realize that a calendar has dates and you don't.

"But I guess I'm not the only one with that problem. The other day, I went to the grocery store. I saw a stock boy and asked if he had any nuts. He said, 'No Ma'am.' Then I said, 'Well, do you have any dates?' He gave me a sorrowful look and said, 'Ma'am, if I don't have nuts, do you really expect me to have dates?'

"I was so desperate, I decided to try Internet dating. That's when I made my first mistake. I thought the international date line was a global dating service.

"Once I had that straightened out, I decided to fill out a dating profile. There's nothing like trying to fill out one of those things to realize how boring you are.

"Nevertheless, a guy saw my profile and swiped right. We went on a date. I found out he was a math teacher. It turned out he was nothing but problems.

"My second date wasn't any better. We started chatting and everything was going great until he told me his career was 'professional blood donor.' I knew right away, he wasn't my type!

"Thank you, folks. It's great to be back."

Acknowledging the applause, Dixie made her way to our table.

Jerry got to his feet and gave her a peck on the cheek. "Great job. I gotta go. I'm up after the next guy."

I thought Dixie would sit. Instead, she leaned over and whispered in my ear. "I'm parched. Performing always makes me thirsty. I'm going to the snack bar to get a soda. Can I get you anything?"

I shook my head. "No, I'm good."

She turned to Kevin. "How about you?"

"Nope. I'm good too."

I watched her weave her way through the crowd as the next comic took the stage.

Dixie was standing in line at the concession stand when she heard someone call her name.

"Ms. Dixie!"

She turned and saw a middle-aged couple behind her. "Yes."

"Hi. We just wanted to tell you how much we loved your routine."

"Oh, well, thanks."

"Any chance we could get your autograph?"

That came as a surprise. She had always gotten compliments, but this was the first time anyone had asked for an autograph.

"Sure, I suppose so."

The man looked back. "I don't want to hold up the line. Maybe if we step over here out of the way you could sign our program?"

Dixie looked wistfully at the soft drink dispenser. She didn't really want to lose her place in line, but she also didn't want to disappoint her fans.

"Okay, why not?"

When they reached a secluded corner, the man said, "I'm afraid we've lured you over here under false pretenses. We're Fred and Myrtle Baxter and we know you're Dixie Smith. We know you are the one who recently had an experience with extraterrestrial beings."

"Look!" Dixie said, "I don't want to talk about that."

She started to move away, but the man grabbed her arm. "Please, just give us a minute and I'll explain."

145

She hesitated. "Okay, but make it quick."

"Thank you," he said, releasing her arm. "We'd like you to join us to celebrate the great conjunction."

"The what? I have no idea what you're talking about."

"Of course you do," he said, smiling. "The conjunction of Jupiter and Saturn. It's tonight! This is the closest conjunction since 1623, the year Shakespeare's collected works were first published. It is the first time in almost 400 years, and it will be 2080 before these two planets align so closely again."

"And that's not all," the woman gushed. "The planet Mars is at its closest to the earth until 2035!"

"I appreciate the history lesson," Dixie said, "but what does all that have to do with me?"

"Don't you see?" the man said, "you are the Chosen One."

"Look," Dixie said, becoming alarmed, "I don't know what you guys are selling, but I'm not interested. I have to get back to my friends."

The man put one hand on her arm and in the other hand she could see he was holding a gun.

"We were afraid you might resist," he said, "so unfortunately we have no choice. Please come with us quietly and no one will get hurt. If you resist, no telling how many innocent bystanders might lose their lives. Before this night is over, you will thank us. We are simply helping you fulfill your destiny."

Reluctantly, Dixie followed the couple to their car. She looked around desperately, and just before the man shoved her into the back seat and climbed in beside her, she thought she saw Walt out of the corner of her eye.

"Where are you taking me?" she asked as they pulled out of the parking lot.

"To the temple," the man replied. "We have built a temple in our home to welcome our friends from the cosmos."

In spite of her worry, Dixie was also curious. "Exactly what are you expecting to happen tonight?"

"The rapture, of course."

"I --- I don't understand."

"It is the fulfillment of prophecy. There are wars and pestilence throughout the world. Mankind has raped Mother Earth. The time for the cleansing has come, just as it did in the days of Noah, only this time, instead of an ark, the faithful will be lifted into the heavens and abide in the Mother Ship while the earth is cleansed with fire."

Dixie was bewildered. "I still don't see what this has to do with me."

"As we said before, you are the Chosen One. The moment we saw your story in the paper, how you were taken up and then returned, we knew you were the one to lead us. Your experience, coming so close to the conjunction of the planets, was our sign that the time had come."

At that moment, the woman turned into a driveway, punched a remote, and pulled into the garage.

"We must hurry!" the man said. "We must be ready when they come."

"Exactly where is this temple you've constructed?" Dixie asked as he led her into the house.

"There's a deck off the bedroom on the second story."

"Outside! It must be forty degrees. We'll freeze!"

"Not to worry," the man said. "You'll be clothed in the royal robes. Myrtle has prepared them."

They led Dixie into a second-floor bedroom. Myrtle went to the closet and pulled out three velvet robes.

She handed one to her husband and one to Dixie.

"The moment we put these on," the man said, "we will no longer be Fred and Myrtle Baxter and you will no longer be Dixie Smith. We will be known by our celestial names. I am Perseus, my wife is Andromeda, and you, the Chosen One, are Cassiopeia."

These people are bat-shit crazy, Dixie thought, *but I'd better play along.*

After the three of them were in their robes, Dixie said, "What now?"

"Now we proceed to the temple, light the welcoming fires, and await the arrival of the Mother Ship."

They led her onto the deck and she watched as they lit oil lamps arranged around the perimeter.

"Just curious," Dixie said. "What happens if nobody shows?"

"They will come," the man replied, resolutely. "We will simply wait here until they do."

"I hope it's soon," Dixie muttered under her breath. "I gotta pee!"

The next comic had just finished when Kevin tapped me on the arm.

"Shouldn't Dixie be back by now?"

"Probably a long line at the concession stand, but you're right. I'll go check."

I made my way through the crowd and was surprised to see that there was no line at the concession stand and no Dixie.

I walked up to the kid wiping the counter.

"Have you seen Dixie Red? She told me she was coming here for a soda."

"Yeah, I saw her," he replied. "She was in line. Then a man and woman came up to her. They talked for a minute then went over to that corner," he said, pointing. "A few minutes later, all three of them left together."

I got a real bad feeling. "How long ago did they leave?"

He shrugged. "Not long. Just a few minutes."

I ran out into the parking lot and spotted them just as a man was shoving Dixie into the back seat of a sedan. Our eyes met for just an instant, then she was gone.

I ran toward the car, but it was already pulling out of the parking lot by the time I got there. I couldn't stop the car, but I did get the number on the license plate.

I pulled out my phone and dialed Ox, my old partner during my five years on the Kansas City Police Force.

"Hey Walt. What's up?"

"Ox, I need you to run a plate for me. A friend of mine has been abducted."

"Sure," he replied, "give me the plate."

I rattled off the number. "And hurry! Please! Her life may be in danger."

I ran back into the club. Jerry had just finished his act and had returned to the table.

"Come on!" I said, "We have to go. Now!"

"But Walt," Jerry protested, "the show isn't over yet." Then he looked around. "Where's Dixie?"

"That's why we've gotta go now!" I muttered. "Someone's taken her!"

We climbed into the car and I explained what I knew while we were waiting for Ox's return call.

I had just finished when my cell rang.

"Walt, I got it. The car is registered to Fred and Myrtle Baxter. The address is on Benton Boulevard. I'll text it to you. Do you want me to come?"

"Yes, and call for back-up. These people might be dangerous."

"Meet you there, partner."

"Fred and Myrtle Baxter?" Kevin said. "That certainly doesn't sound like the names of hired assassins."

"But who else could it be?" Jerry wailed. "How far away is their address?"

I looked at my phone. "Benton Boulevard. About fifteen minutes."

"Then let's go!" Jerry urged. "Hurry!"

We pulled up in front of an old two-story with an attached garage. We couldn't see any lights from where we were sitting.

"We don't even know if they brought her here," Kevin said.

"Only one way to find out."

The overhead door wouldn't budge.

"Probably has an automatic opener," Kevin whispered. "Let's look for another way in."

We went around the side and found a regular door leading into the garage. It was locked too.

"Kevin," I whispered, "do you have your picks?"

"Does Mr. Spock have pointed ears?" he replied, reaching into his pocket.

A moment later, we were inside.

"They're here," Kevin said, putting his hand on the car hood. "It's still warm."

I tried the door into the house. It was unlocked.

I turned to Jerry. "You stay here while we check things out."

"The hell I will!" he replied, indignantly. "That's my girlfriend in there."

I looked at Kevin and he just shrugged.

"Okay, but be quiet."

Kevin and I pulled our guns and we headed into the house. No one was on the first floor. I pointed to the stairway and Kevin nodded.

We tiptoed up the stairs and saw a light coming from one of the rooms on the back of the house.

I peeked into the room. It was empty, but there was a glow coming from a deck on the back of the house. I slipped into the room and motioned for Kevin and Jerry to follow.

We saw three figures in the glow of kerosene lamps. They were all dressed in some kind of fancy robes. One of them had to be Dixie.

"Ready?" I whispered.

Kevin nodded.

We stepped onto the deck. "Everyone! Freeze and hands in the air."

"Walt! Thank God!" Dixie moaned. "Be careful. The guy has a gun."

We frisked the guy, relieved him of his weapon, and ushered everyone inside.

The minute Jerry saw Dixie, he rushed to her side. "Are you okay?"

"I am --- now. Thanks to you guys."

"What's with the fancy duds?" Kevin asked.

Dixie relayed the whole story from the moment she was accosted in the club.

"You gotta be kidding!" Kevin said. "That's the craziest story I've ever heard."

At that moment, Ox and two more officers came into the room, weapons drawn.

He looked at us all in bewilderment.

"What the hell?"

I pointed to the two kidnappers. "Ox this is Perseus and Andromeda. Read them their rights."

After they were led away in cuffs, Dixie said, "I'll be right with you guys. I gotta pee."

As we were waiting for Dixie to heed the call of Mother Nature, I thought I saw a shaft of bright light illuminate the deck.

It was just there for a moment and then it was gone.

Maybe it was just my imagination.

CHAPTER 16

A few days after her unfortunate encounter with Fred and Myrtle Baxter, I received a call from Dixie.

"Walt, what do you know about MUFON?"

"I know they're quite tasty. We get them from HyVee. Maggie likes the poppyseed. I prefer the chocolate chip."

"No, no! Not muffins! MUFON, the Mutual UFO Network. Ever heard of them?"

"Can't say that I have. Why do you ask?"

"I received a call from them this morning. They want to interview me."

"I thought you'd decided to stay away from anything UFO related."

"I did --- but they said I have a story that should be shared with the world. They were very convincing."

"So what did you tell them?"

"I agreed to an interview --- just to hear what they have to say. It's tomorrow morning at ten o'clock here at the trailer. I'd like you be there if you can."

"Sure, I'd be happy to."

After I hung up from Dixie, I fired up the old Toshiba and Googled MUFON.

I read on Wikipedia that the Mutual UFO Network is a US-based non-profit organization composed of civilian volunteers who study reported UFO sightings. It is one of the oldest and largest organizations of its kind, claiming more than 4,000 members worldwide with chapters and representatives in more than 43 countries and all 50 states.

Based in California, it holds annual symposiums and publishes the monthly *MUFON UFO Journal*. It also has an online UFO university where it trains members to report UFO sightings. It has a website which features a newsroom and case management system.

I also read that the organization had come under fire from reputable scientists who claim their work is pseudoscience and spawns outlandish conspiracy theories. Not surprisingly, it is claimed that many of MUFON's supporters fall on the far right of the political spectrum.

I pulled up the MUFON webpage and was immediately impressed with its professional appearance.

In its welcoming statement I read: *"Our goal is to be the inquisitive minds' refuge seeking answers to that most ancient question, "Are we alone in the universe?" The answer very simply, is NO. Whether you have UFO reports to share, armchair UFO investigator aspirations, or want to train and join our investigation team, MUFON is here for you. Won't you please join us in our quest to discover the truth?"*

The page was filled with videos and reports of sightings and encounters by its members.

If a person was a UFO buff, this definitely was the place to be.

I found myself actually looking forward to our meeting tomorrow.

I arrived at Dixie's trailer thirty minutes before our scheduled meeting.

Not surprisingly, Dixie was in a dither.

"Walt! Am I crazy having these people here? I said I didn't want any publicity, and here I am, inviting the largest UFO organization in the world into my home."

"Calm down. All we're doing today is listening to their pitch. You haven't agreed to anything yet. If you don't like what they have to say, you can send them packing. No harm, no foul."

She wrung her hands. "I suppose that's true, but I keep thinking about that creepy Michael Sullivan. What if the powerful people he was talking about find out what I'm doing?"

"Yes, there is that to consider, but like I said, you haven't done anything yet. Let's just listen. Then you can make a decision."

At that moment, there was a knock on the front door.

She shuddered. "They're here!"

I put my hand on her arm. "Take a deep breath. I'm right here with you."

When she opened the door, a young man introduced himself.

"Ms. Smith, My name is Martin Hopkins and this is my associate, Cynthia Street. We're from MUFON. So happy to finally meet you."

"Please come in," she replied, stepping aside. She pointed at me. "This is a friend of mine, Walter Williams. I asked him to meet with us today. I hope you don't mind."

"Of course not," he said, extending his hand. "We have no secrets to hide."

Once we were seated, Hopkins said, "I'd like to begin by telling you about our organization."

In the next ten minutes, he shared the same information that I had gleaned from the Internet.

After he finished, he said, "Do you have any questions so far."

I raised my hand. "I do. I read pretty much everything you just shared on the Internet. I also read that your organization has its share of detractors."

He smiled. "You got that right. The amazing thing, is that in spite of the thousands of sightings throughout the world and reports of encounters like Ms. Smith experienced, the U.S. government as well as most other governments, stubbornly insist that we are alone in the universe and that there never has been and never will be, contact from alien civilizations.

"With that antiquated view, it's not surprising that scientists whose projects are funded by government grants are more than willing to say that our claims are preposterous and that our methods are pseudoscience.

"It's also common knowledge that the press is owned by the political elite. They print what they're told to print and ignore what they're told to ignore. Unfortunately, the concept of a free press is a thing of the past.

"That's why organizations like ours exist --- to share the truth to the world."

"A lofty goal," I replied, "but isn't it a bit dangerous to contradict the official stance of the U.S. government?"

I saw the look of concern on his face.

"Have you been contacted by someone from the government?"

I nodded. "Tell him, Dixie."

In the next ten minutes, she shared her frightening visit from Michael Sullivan that ended with the dire warning that it would be in her best interests to retract her statement.

"After she refused," I added, "it was just a few days until the brakes on her car mysteriously failed. Thankfully she wasn't hurt --- this time."

Hopkins and his partner exchanged a grave look. "I'm so sorry to hear that. It's the political process at its worst. Intimidation and coercion used to control the narrative to the public.

"You may or not be aware that after the Roswell incident, the military retracted its statement about a crashed UFO and claimed it was merely a weather balloon."

"Yes, I'm familiar with that scenario," I replied.

"What you may not know," he continued, "was that every member of the military that was involved in the Roswell incident was instructed in no uncertain terms, never to speak of what they'd seen. In fact, that gag order was expanded to include all of the military by virtue of the Espionage Act of 1953. The act made it a crime for anyone in the military to disclose UFO evidence to the public."

"It's inconceivable," Cynthia continued, "that for seventy years, the government has been lying to its citizens about the existence of extraterrestrial visitations."

"But why?" I asked.

"Consider the possibility that there was actually a crash of a UFO at Roswell. In fact, consider the possibility that there were other less publicized crashes that the government covered up. Imagine that alien technology was recovered that was far beyond anything we currently have. It is suspected that the military has recovered such technology and is working on retrofitting what they found in secret bases like Roswell. It is even suspected that live alien beings have been recovered and are working with our military."

"See!" Dixie blurted. "That's exactly what I saw when the alien placed his hands on my head!"

Our visitors were startled. "You actually saw that? How?"

"If you don't mind me using Star Trek as an example," I said, "it's very much like the collective consciousness of the Borg. What one knows, everyone knows. When the alien placed his hands on Dixie's head, it was like some kind of Vulcan mind meld. She knew what the alien knew. It was just for a second, but it was there."

"Incredible!" Hopkins gushed. "This is exactly the kind of thing that we should be sharing with the world."

Cynthia took Dixie by the hand. "Would you be willing to go public with your story? We'd love to put it on our website."

"I can go you one better," Hopkins said. "Based on what you've just described, I'm quite confident that the *History Channel* would feature your story on their *Ancient Alien* series. What do you say?"

Dixie shook her head. "I'm not sure I want to become the poster girl for senior citizen abductees. It seems that kind of publicity would put a price on my head. Michael Sullivan or one of his goons would be certain to come after me."

"Not necessarily," Hopkins replied. "Right now, if you suddenly disappeared, only Walt and your other close friends would know or care. The world doesn't know Dixie Smith, but once you're on our website and on TV, everyone will know and it will make it very difficult for them to come after you."

"I don't know," I replied. "Just look at Julian Assange with Wikileaks and Edward Snowden. They're prominent figures but that hasn't stopped the government from going after them."

"Apples and oranges," Hopkins replied. "The government doesn't have them on some kind of 'hit list.' They're going after them through legal channels for espionage and treason.

"As much as they may not like what Dixie has to say, it's certainly a far cry from treason."

"That may be," Dixie said, "but I'll never forget the look in Sullivan's eyes when he told me that I had pissed off some very powerful people."

"Look," Cynthia said, "We're not saying that there's no risk at all. We can't promise that. May I ask your age?"

"I'm no spring chicken. I'm seventy-five."

"I want you to ask yourself, in all those years, have you ever done anything that would have a lasting and profound effect on your fellow man?"

Dixie closed her eyes and I guessed she was thinking about all those years as a stripper, a magician's girl Friday, an extra in B movies, and a stand-up comic.

"No," she finally replied. "I guess I haven't."

"Well," Cynthia said, "This is your chance. How many women, especially a woman your age, have had the opportunity to make a real impact in people's lives?"

She nodded. "I think I see your point."

Hopkins leaned forward expectantly. "Then you'll do it?"

Dixie nodded. "I will! I'm in!"

At that moment I remembered my role in being there. I was to be the voice of caution.

"Dixie, are you sure? Once your story is on the Internet and the *History Channel*, there's no turning back. The cat's out of the bag."

"I don't care," she replied resolutely. "I'm seventy-five. No telling how many years I have left. Probably not a lot. If they get me, they get me. At least I'll go out in a blaze of glory!"

"Fantastic!" Hopkins gushed, clapping his hands. "How about two days from now. We can have our crew here by then and begin filming."

"Works for me!" she replied. "I'm actually anxious to get started."

I wasn't the least bit excited. I had no idea how I was going to tell Jerry that his girlfriend had just placed herself in the crosshairs of government assassins.

CHAPTER 17

Dixie opened her closet door and began shuffling through the hangers of clothing.

"Nope! Not a chance! Yuck, where did I get that? You've got to be kidding me."

"Well damn! Out of all these clothes, not a single thing to wear for my interview. The last thing I want, is to look like Angela Lansbury on *Murder She Wrote*. Guess I'd better head to the mall and buy some new threads."

Dixie climbed into her car and headed to the Macy's department store at the Independence Center shopping mall.

She had just stepped out of her car when she heard a voice behind her.

"Good morning, Dixie."

She turned, and to her horror, saw Michael Sullivan and two other guys with shaved heads and bulging muscles.

"What --- what do you want?"

Sullivan smiled. "Why you, of course. We know about your upcoming interview with those idiots from MUFON and we just can't let that happen."

"How do you know about that?"

"Please Dixie, give us some credit. It's our job to know these things. I gave you a chance to retract your story or at the very least, keep your mouth shut, but unfortunately, you've chosen to ignore my warning. Now you must face the consequences. Get in the van --- now!"

"I don't care who you are!" she replied defiantly. "I'm a U.S. citizen and I have rights! You can't just ---."

"Oh, but we can. Sometimes sacrifices must be made for the greater good."

"What are you going to do to me?"

"Unfortunately, you are going to suffer a heart attack. It's not at all uncommon for people your age. One injection of potassium chloride will do the trick. After the deed is done, we'll simply return your lifeless body here to your car. Some passing shopper will find your body slumped over the steering wheel. Now get in the van!"

Dixie looked around frantically, hoping to call out for help, but no one was in sight.

When she didn't move, Sullivan motioned to the two goons behind him. "Look, Dixie, we can either do this the easy way or the hard way, but one way or the other, you're getting in this van. Your choice."

Seeing the two brutes step forward, she realized that a struggle would be in vain and possibly very painful.

"Okay, I'll get in, but you're not going to get away with this. I have friends."

"Indeed you do, and I'm sure they'll be devastated to hear that your poor old heart just gave out."

They drove to a rural farmhouse and led Dixie to a shed behind the house.

"Make yourself comfortable," Sullivan said. "The doc will be here in about an hour to take care of things."

After they closed and locked the door, Dixie took stock of her surroundings. There was nothing in the shed but one hard-backed chair. There was only one window and it was barred.

She sighed. "Just one more hour to live. I'll be damned if I'm going to spend it sitting in that hard chair."

She went to the window and peered out. *Freedom,* she thought. *So near, and yet so far away.*

Suddenly, a shaft of light shot through the window illuminating the dim interior of the shed. A peaceful feeling came over her as the light enveloped her body. She felt the weightlessness as her body began lifting off the floor. She closed her eyes in peaceful slumber.

It was just past noon on the day after our meeting with the people from MUFON. I was about to lay down for a quick snooze when the phone rang. It was Georgia.

"Walt, have you heard from Dixie today?"

"No, why do you ask?"

"She called me last night and told me about your visit yesterday and her upcoming interview. She wanted me and Granny Smith to be there too. I tried to reach her this morning, but got no answer. Each time I called, it went straight to voice mail.

"I was concerned, so I drove out to her trailer. She wasn't there and her car was gone. It's been four hours and I'm starting to get worried."

"Any chance she could be shopping? I know you gals get all in a dither wanting to look just right."

"I guess that's possible, but that doesn't explain why she isn't answering her phone."

"Maybe the battery's dead and she forgot to charge it."

"Yeah --- maybe. Anyway, I'm worried. If she did go shopping, it would be at the Independence Center Mall. I think I'll drive out there and look around."

"Sounds like a plan. Let me know if you find anything."

An hour and a half later, Georgia called again.

"Walt, I found Dixie's car at the mall. I've been in every store and there's no sign of her. I even had the mall office call for her over the intercom. She's just not here."

"Where's her car?"

"Outside the Macy's store on the east side."

"I'll meet you there."

I spotted Georgia standing beside Dixie's car.

"Still nothing?" I asked.

She shook her head. "Nothing."

I thought for a moment. "Obviously she drove here, but if she never made it inside, it sounds like she might have run into trouble out here in the parking lot."

I looked around and spotted a surveillance camera on the corner of the building. It seemed to be pointing in our direction.

"Come on," I said, "I have an idea."

I knew from my days on the force that there was an Independence police office in the mall.

We entered, and I presented my card to the officer on duty.

"My name is Walt Williams. I'm a private investigator, but I spent five years on the job with Kansas City. I need your help."

He looked at the card. "Walt Williams. That name rings a bell." Then he grinned. "Are you the old guy who started that C.R.A.P. program and worked with a big guy they call Ox?"

"Yep, that's me."

"What can I do for you, Walt?"

"A friend of ours has gone missing. Her car is in the lot outside of Macy's. We think it's possible she may have been abducted. I spotted a video camera on the building. Any chance we could take a look at the footage?"

"Absolutely," he replied. "Let me pull up that camera."

He fiddled with the equipment while we watched the screen.

"Here you go," he said. "Which car is hers?"

I pointed it out.

"Okay, then. I'll just back track until we see her pull up."

"There," I said. "That's her."

The time stamp said 10:00.

"Son-of-a-bitch!" the cop muttered, as we watched Dixie being accosted by three men. "Do you recognize any of these guys?"

I didn't, but I had a pretty good idea who they were.

After a few minutes, Dixie was herded into a van and they drove away.

"Damn! No license plate!" the cop said. "I'll put out an APB on the van. What's your friend's name?"

"Dixie Smith."

"I have your card. I'll give you a call if we come up with anything."

"What now?" Georgia asked as we left the police office.

"I have no idea. We can't just go roaming around. They could be anywhere."

"Who do you think took her?" Georgia asked, wiping a tear from her eye.

"My guess, it was some government goons. They must have gotten wind of her upcoming exposé and just couldn't let it happen."

"I'm going back to the trailer," she said. "Maybe she --- or someone else might call. I don't know what else to do."

I didn't either. "Want some company?"

"Sure."

We got back to the trailer just as the sun was setting. Georgia found a couple of soft drinks in the fridge and we just sat there, hoping for the best, but fearing the worst.

We had been sitting there maybe thirty minutes when we heard the back door open.

A moment later, Dixie walked into the room.

"Aunt Dix!" Georgia shouted, throwing her arms around her. "You're safe! Thank God!"

"Of course I'm safe," Dixie replied, prying Georgia away. "Why wouldn't I be? And why are you two in my living room? I didn't hear you come in."

Georgia and I just stood there with our mouths hanging open.

"Where have you been?" Georgia finally asked. "We've been so worried about you."

"I can't imagine why you'd be worried. I just went out on the back porch to watch the sunset, then I come in and you two are in my living room."

"Aunt Dix!" Georgia protested, "what about your abduction?"

She looked at us like we were out of our minds.

"I have no idea what you're talking about."

CHAPTER 18

For the next hour, we quizzed Dixie about everything that had transpired since her abduction by the aliens. She remembered nothing. She didn't remember being taken into the space ship, the visit from Michael Sullivan, the visit from the folks from MUFON, her abduction in the mall parking lot --- nothing! As far as she was concerned, it was as if none of it had ever happened.

Our only conclusion, as far-fetched as it seemed, was that she had once again been taken by the aliens and that they had somehow wiped her memory of the past few weeks. It was the only logical explanation of how she had escaped the government assassins and returned with no memory of what had transpired.

The moment I was convinced that her memory was truly gone, I called Mark Davenport.

"Mark, Walt here. You'd better sit down because you're not going to believe the story I'm about to tell you."

For the next fifteen minutes, I shared the weird series of events that had transpired.

"So," I concluded, "here's what I want you to do. Get in touch with whatever clandestine agency is trying to silence Dixie and tell them to call off their dogs. She has absolutely no memory of any alien abduction, so there's no need to make her disappear. Can you do that?"

For a few minutes there was no reply. "Walt, if anyone else had told me this story, I would have said they're bat-shit crazy. Let me make a call. I'll see what I can do."

Fifteen minutes later, Mark called back.

"Everything's on hold --- for now, pending my investigation."

"Investigation?"

"Come on Walt. Do you think for a minute these guys are going to take your word that Dixie has forgotten everything? You have to admit, your story is quite a stretch. I'm going to catch the red eye to Kansas City. I'll talk to Dixie myself and if I'm satisfied that she's no longer a threat, that will be the last of it."

"Fantastic! See you tomorrow."

When Mark arrived, he began by asking Dixie a few simple questions. Naturally, she didn't understand what all the fuss was about, but she was willing to play along to keep us all happy.

"Would you object to taking a polygraph?" Mark asked.

Dixie grinned. "It's okay as long as you don't ask any questions about my sex life."

Mark laughed. "No, I assure you. Nothing like that."

He hooked her up and for the next twenty minutes he grilled her about everything connected to her encounter with the extraterrestrials. Naturally, she remembered nothing.

When he finished, he shrugged. "Looks like we're done here. She seems to be telling the truth."

Then I remembered one more thing that I thought might put the icing on the cake.

"Dixie, would you mind going with us to see Doc Johnson?"

"Who's Doc Johnson?"

Dopey me. Of course she wouldn't remember him.

"He took an x-ray of your foot. I'd like to have him take another for comparison."

She shrugged. "Sure, if that will help put an end to all this nonsense."

I made a call to set up the appointment and on the way to Doc's office I told Mark about the implant we had found.

Doc Johnson took the second x-ray and we watched breathlessly as the image popped up on his computer screen.

"Here," he said, "is the first x-ray."

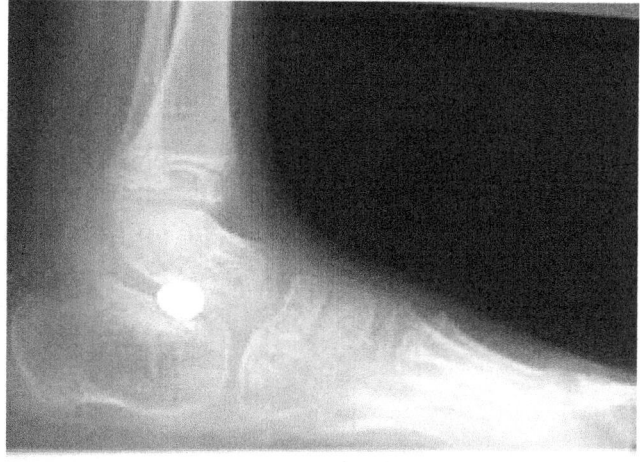

"And this is the one I just took."

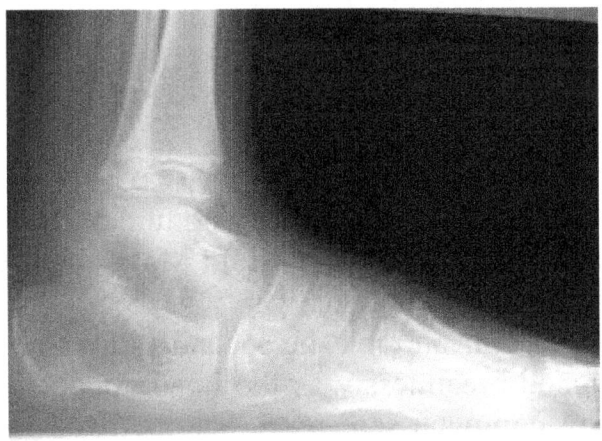

"Well, I'll be damned," Mark muttered. "It's gone!"

"Do you think you have enough evidence to take to Washington?"

"I do," he replied. "You have my word that Dixie is no longer in danger."

"Thank God!" Dixie sighed. "Can I go home now?"

EPILOGUE

Needless to say, the folks from MUFON were bummed that they weren't going to get the juicy story of Dixie's abduction to publish on their website.

I couldn't tell them the truth. If they had a clue that she had been abducted a second time, they would have continued to hound her. I simply told them that after she had time to think it over, that she'd had a change of heart. With the threat of persecution by the government hanging over her head, it just wasn't worth the risk.

Jerry, on the other hand, was absolutely thrilled that his new sweetie was out of the national spotlight and the cross hairs of covert assassins, and back in the spotlight of the Comedy Club.

And speaking of assassins, what happened to Dixie is absolutely frightening.

While I have no problem at all with Uncle Sam taking out the likes of Osama Bin Laden or homegrown terrorists like the two brothers that set off bombs during the Boston Marathon, I have a real problem with the government making folks disappear just to cover up their dirty little secrets.

I guess it was some kind of cosmic karma that the very thing that got Dixie in Dutch to begin with, saved her life in the end.

Over the years, I've marveled that Lady Justice has been able to use old guys like me, hookers, con men, and a host of other unlikely characters to keep the scales of justice balanced. How cool to know that she's also able to enlist visitors from the cosmos to keep the bad guys in check.

Poor Dixie.

In the few months I'd known her, she had been abducted five times, once by Sammy Spalitto, once by the goofy Perseus and Andromeda, once by government assassins, and twice by our alien visitors.

Thankfully, the only one she remembers is the abduction by Spalitto, and that one didn't turn out too bad.

But seeing what the poor woman went through made me realize one thing.

My name is Walt Williams and if I'm ever abducted by aliens, I swear I'll never tell a living soul!

ABOUT THE AUTHOR

   Award-winning author, Robert Thornhill, began writing at the age of sixty-six and in eleven short years has penned forty-four novels in the Lady Justice mystery/comedy series, the seven volume Rainbow Road series of chapter books for children, a cookbook and a mini-autobiography.

   Lady Justice and the Sting, Lady Justice and Dr. Death, Lady Justice and the Vigilante, Lady Justice and the Candidate, Lady Justice and the Book Club Murders, Lady Justice and the Cruise Ship Murders and *Lady Justice and the Vet* won the Pinnacle Award for the best new mystery novels of Fall 2011, Winter 2012, Summer 2012, Fall 2012, Spring of 2013 and Summer 2014 from the National Association of Book Entrepreneurs.

   Many of Walt's adventures in the Lady Justice series are anecdotal and based on Robert's real life.

   Although Robert holds a master's in psychology, he has never taken a course in writing and has never learned to type. All 53 of his published books were typed with one finger and a thumb!

   His wit and insight come from his varied occupations, including thirty-three years as a real estate broker. He lives with his wife, Peg, in Independence, Missouri.

   Visit him on the Web at: http://BooksByBob.com

The Lady Justice Series
is now 44 volumes of mystery and laughs.

Every volume is available on Kindle and is enrolled
in Kindle Unlimited.
See them all here:
https://amzn.to/2JizoqS

****
Every volume is available on audio
See them all here:
https://adbl.co/2NuUBmq

****
If you prefer to hold a real book in your hand,
See the paperbacks here:
http://booksbybob.com

****
The Rainbow Road Series
of children's chapter books

See them all here:
http://bit.ly/2Ln4Ab3

Volume #1
Lady Justice Takes a C.R.A.P.

http://amzn.to/16lfjnY

****

Volume #2
Lady Justice and the Lost Tapes

amzn.to/1twzOfq

****

Volume #3
Lady Justice Gets Lei'd

http://amzn.to/15P6bLg

Volume #4
Lady Justice and the Avenging Angels

****

Volume #4
Lady Justice and the Sting

****
*

Volume #6
Lady Justice and Dr. Death

Volume #7
Lady Justice and the Vigilante

http://amzn.to/1d3FLK6

****

Volume #8
Lady Justice and the Watchers

http://amzn.to/15P5LEE

****

Volume #9
Lady Justice and the Candidate

http://amzn.to/19f3XVZ

Volume #10
Lady Justice and the Book Club Murders

http://amzn.to/1aWGg3K

****

Volume #11
Lady Justice and the Cruise Ship Murders

http://amzn.to/16VjURw

****

Volume #12
Lady Justice and the Class Reunion

http://amzn.to/17S9YE0

Volume #13
Lady Justice and the Assassin

http://amzn.to/1bDdrKJ

****

Volume #14
Lady Justice and the Lottery

http://amzn.to/1exhji6

****

Volume #15
Lady Justice and the Vet

http://amzn.to/17GyE3n

Volume #16
Lady Justice and the Organ Traders

amzn.to/1jmde5S

****

Volume #17
Lady Justice and the Pharaoh's Curse

http://amzn.to/1yHlnGE

****

Volume #18
Lady Justice in the Eye of the Storm

amzn.to/1w6CthZ

Volume #19
Lady Justice on the Dark Side

amzn.to/1LFIDyS

****

Volume #20
Lady Justice and the Broken Hearts

http://amzn.to/1I1xTIW

****

Volume #21
Lady Justice and the Conspiracy

http://amzn.to/1Ms5KLR

Volume #22
Lady Justice and the Conspiracy Trial

http://amzn.to/23vfry5

****

Volume #23
Lady Justice and the Ghostly Treasure

http://amzn.to/235rVO9

****

Volume #24
Lady Justice and the Ghost Whisperer

http://amzn.to/2cwzNU6

Volume #25
Lady Justice and the Spy

****

Volume #26
Lady Justice and the Cat

****

Volume #27
Lady Justice and the Geriatric Gumshoes

Volume #28
Lady Justice and the Sixth Sense

http://amzn.to/2DCdQFj

****

Volume #29
Lady Justice and the Magic Dragon

http://amzn.to/2FRJ5te

****

Volume #30
Lady Justice and the Black Widow

https://amzn.to/2Juo2lz

Volume #31
Lady Justice and the Devil's Breath

https://amzn.to/2Nxw5fJ

****
*

Volume #32
Lady Justice and the Mysterious Box

https://amzn.to/2CrzlsC

****

Volume #33
Lady Justice and the Mystery Mansion

https://amzn.to/2rYkSfk

Volume #34
Lady Justice and Good vs Evil

https://amzn.to/2GxixAx

****

Volume #35
Lady Justice and the Quirky Arlo Quimby

https://amzn.to/2EGgnMp

****
*

Volume #36
Lady Justice and the Evil Twin

https://amzn.to/2vSzlvk

Volume #37
Lady Justice and the Living Trust

https://amzn.to/2Lrdnsm
****

Volume #38
Lady Justice and the Bad Seed

https://amzn.to/2HuogXM

Volume #39
Lady Justice and the Raven

https://amzn.to/2uCUeNU

Volume #40
Lady Justice and the Landlords' Nightmare

https://amzn.to/2VatcZm

****

Volume #41
Lady Justice and Terror on the Tracks

https://amzn.to/2x10wZ1

****

Volume #42
Lady Justice and the Bounty Hunter

https://amzn.to/3e1Zf3V

Volume #43
Lady Justice Down on the Farm

https://amzn.to/3gHGIvl

Made in the USA
Middletown, DE
24 January 2021

32315163R00116